The Author

MORDECAI RICHLER was born in Montreal, Quebec, in 1931. Raised there in the working-class Jewish neighbourhood around St. Urbain Street, he attended Sir George Williams College (now a part of Concordia University). In 1951 he left Canada for Europe, settling in London, England, in 1954. Eighteen years later, he moved back to Montreal.

Novelist and journalist, screenwriter and editor, Richler, one of our most acclaimed writers, spent much of his career chronicling, celebrating, and criticizing the Montreal and the Canada of his youth. Whether the settings of his fiction are St. Urbain Street or European capitals, his major characters never forsake the Montreal world that shaped them. His most frequent voice is that of the satirist, rendering an honest account of his times with care and humour.

Richler's many honours included the Giller Prize, two Governor General's Awards, and innumerable other awards for fiction, journalism, and screenwriting.

Mordecai Richler died in Montreal in 2001.

Mordecai Richler

THE ACROBATS

With an Afterword by Ted Kotcheff

M&S

Copyright © 1954 by Mordecai Richler
Copyright © 2002 by Mordecai Richler Productions, Inc.
Afterword copyright © 2002 by Ted Kotcheff

This book was first published by André Deutsch Limited in 1954
New Canadian Library edition 2002

National Library of Canada Cataloguing in Publication Data

Richler, Mordecai, 1931–2001
The acrobats / Mordecai Richler ; with an afterword by Ted Kotcheff.

(New Canadian library)
ISBN 0-7710-3478-4

I. Title. II. Series.

PS8535.I38A7 2002   c813'.54   C2002-901347-X
PR9199.3.R3A7 2002

We acknowledge the financial support of the Government of Canada through the Book Publishing Industry Development Program for our publishing activities. We further acknowledge the support of the Canada Council for the Arts and the Ontario Arts Council for our publishing program.

Typesetting by M&S, Toronto
Printed and bound in Canada

McClelland & Stewart Ltd.
The Canadian Publishers
481 University Avenue
Toronto, Ontario
M5G 2E9
www.mcclelland.com/NCL

1 2 3 4 5   06 05 04 03 02

The Acrobats

BOOK ONE

Fué un tiempo de mentira, de infamia. A España toda,
la malherida España, de Carnaval vestida
nos la pusieron, pobre y escuálida y beoda,
para que no acertara la mano con la herida.

ANTONIO MACHADO

It was a time of lies, of infamy. They put our Spain,
That sorely wounded Spain, in Carnival dress,
And then they made her poor, squalid and drunken,
So that no hand should touch the open wound.

I

SPRAWLED OUT on the terrace of Café Ruzafa, Barney felt uneasy now that the afternoon sun glared into his eyes. His face was not so much childish as prematurely aged but still unformed: also irreverent, as if his presence in the Colosseum would have been sufficient to render it into a baseball stadium. His eyes gleamed with something of the innocence and awkward aspirations of the American. He was wearing a tan gabardine suit and a loud bow tie. His pink hands rested dumbly on the table, curled up in hairless balls.

He was sorry. He wasn't going to remind her again how much money the trip was costing him, how the business was floundering without him around to look after his own interests.

An emaciated girl with hollow dark eyes and probably no more than seven years appeared suddenly at their table, the palm of her dirty hand outstretched. She looked at him. Not smiling, not frowning. He tried to ignore her.

Jessie puckered up her cherry lips impatiently. "Oh, do give her something, Barney. People are watching us."

"I don't give a damn about the money. But if I give her something in a minute every bum in town will be down on me."

There were two bulging circles under the girl's eyes. Her palm still silently outstretched she scratched a pimple on her cheek with her free hand.

"Barney! Will you please please do something. She smells so badly. She must have fleas!"

Barney pulled out his damp linen handkerchief again and mopped his forehead. As soon as he was finished, new beads of sweat began to form.

"You think this kid is poor, huh? I bet her pop owns stacks of property all over town. The whole thing is a racket. They know just too damn well what suckers we all are."

"People are watching us!"

Barney glared at Derek, hoping for support.

"*Merde, alors!* Give the brat her *centimos.*" Immediately, Derek was sorry for having said "*merde, alors.*" Why try to impress Barney? "Perhaps she's an orphan? Think of it, *amigo.* Her proletarian papa died for freedom." Derek, his eyes sick with mockery, pretended the table was a drum. He began to tap out *Freiheit* with his fingers. His voice was solemn. "On that day, the day he fell, the sun was high in the sky, all was quiet along the Manzanares. El Campesino clapped him on the shoulder. Comrade, he said, the fate of Madrid is in your hands. Go get us Mola! Juan gritted his teeth. He was pleased with his mission. With him, or under him, was his faithful stallion, Trigger. *No pasarán*, he said grimly. Then, as he galloped off into the setting sun, MGM cameras grinding madly, a fascist sniper laid him flat with three quick shots in the buttocks. Fade out. And today his only child, a street urchin destined for stardom in '60, begs alms from the American *nouveaux-riches.*"

Jessie applauded. "Whee!" she said.

Barney selected a few *centimos* from his loose change and pressed it into the child's filthy hand. I had to bring along her good-for-nothing brother too, he thought. Mr. D.T.'s in person. And I've yet to see the day when that cheapskate will pick up a bill.

Here, on this dilapidated street of cafés, theatres, and hotels, between the Plaza de Torros and the Plaza del Caudillo, all of Valencia appeared to be passing in lazy procession.

Many primlipped girls paraded about in the traditional costumes. Their dresses were hoopskirted and coloured like
candysticks. The girls floated down the street as if secretly
afraid that at any moment they might topple over. This year
the *Fallera Mayor* was the homely daughter of the Minister
of Education. Her attendants included the daughters of the
Mayor of Valencia, a veteran of the Blue Division. Visitors to
the city were taking advantage of the holiday to shop. Many
a sorry husband toddled along after his puffy wife, hidden
under mountains of parcels and souvenirs, perpetually
exposed to ridicule from more masterful men who guzzled
wine on shady terraces whilst their wives fussed to no avail
opposite them, perhaps sipping a warm *gaseosa*. Ragged guitarists serenaded the tourists and leered for the occasional
snapshot, cunning children of the poor played an earnest
game of tag in and out amongst the crowd, lifting wallets on
their way, sluts bargained here and there with fading gallants,
and the aloof bourgeois in their mean black suits, sweating,
unimpressed, just a bit too conscious of the stink of other
bodies, idled about glumly, their pious wives dangling like
dumplings from their sides.

The children felt time lag painfully until night would fall
and again there would be a gigantic display of fireworks. The
ineffectual revolutionaries continued to plot and groan, but
they drank more and sang their songs in lustier voices. Police,
spies, guards, continued to move among them.

Barney tried to interest himself in the passing women, but
all he could think of was that time and money wasted kept
adding up, that the whole trip, contrary to his calculations,
wasn't helping things any. Through eight years of marriage it
had always been nag nag nag – why? because he had unfail-
ingly insisted that a dollar in the bank was just that much
wiser living than a dollar spent. She wanted to look up her
worthless brother – okay! But now his investment wasn't
paying off. And that's dangerous, he thought. For there are the

kids. Mary Anne, six; Sheldon, four. And Jessie, he had to admit, looked pretty and said bright things when he was obliged to take so-and-so and his wife out for dinner.

"*Garçon!*" Jessie yelled. "More coniak!"

Derek frowned. "They're not *garçons* in Spain."

"Maybe we shouldn't have anything more to drink before supper?" Barney said.

"Why?" Jessie asked. "Can you think of anything else to do in this half-assed town?"

"Well we could look at the fireworks."

"Boom! Bam! Pszzt!" Derek twisted his weak handsome face so that his dimples showed. "I'm tired of fireworks."

"Wook at the ity-pretty menses working on the big figure in the square."

"That's the major falla," Barney said earnestly. "It's supposed to represent a Valencian of the Middle Ages."

"*Falya*, not falla," Derek said absently.

"Okay! Fine. Falyah!"

"Derek isn't the falyah so pwetty? Awen't you gwad we came?"

"One, I'm not glad we came. I find the two of you absolutely boring." His eyes, deeply set and wild from drink, shone like buttons. "Two, I don't find the *falla* pretty. Even as a symbol it's gross, uncultured."

"It seems silly," Barney said. "They spend a whole week making 'em and then they burn 'em in one night. Not that they don't clean up enough on a fiesta anyway. But why make something only to burn it? It doesn't seem practical."

Derek lit a cigarette. He tossed his head back with studied abandon and blew a big puff of smoke into the still air. I shouldn't have come back, he thought. It was wrong.

"You know what?" There was a taunt in Jessie's eyes, and her voice was unnaturally thick. "He thinks I'm going to get high and maybe go to bed with a cute Spaniard. Don't you, *honey-bunny*?"

Barney faked a laugh. "Now don't be silly, dear."

"Watsamatter? Don't you think they're cute?"

"Of course they're cute."

"You see, Derek, he thinks they're cute."

"He's a fairy," Derek said obligingly.

"Derek says you're a fairy, dear."

"I heard him, *dear*."

"Aren't you going to do anything?"

"Can't you stop for just two minutes?" Derek asked. "Let's order another round of drinks."

"I think maybe we've all had plenty to drink."

Jessie stared at him with a knowing disgust – an emotion that was the flux of a degenerated intimacy; an intimacy of smelly socks, after-dinner burping, sleeping noises, soiled underwear, and dental odours. Barney avoided her eyes: it was a look he had come to dread. She shuddered. "Are you worried about the business, dear?" she asked dryly.

"No!"

Jessie pointed a slender, elegantly manicured finger at the man who was seated alone at another table. "Oh, look at the cute fairy with the sketch book!" The man was young. He had a lean, bony head. His brown and brooding eyes stared ahead vacantly, probing for something apart, inwards, as if they had temporarily rejected reality. He sat absolutely still, rigidly so, and Jessie recognised the posture as a painful discipline. "Look, Derek! Can't you see him?"

"I don't like the expression on his face," Derek said. "It's strictly St. Germain-des-Prés. Holy Christ, look at him! I'm sick of being judged by sensitive adolescents."

"He's cute."

"They all are," Barney said, winking, overjoyed that someone other than himself had succeeded in employing their malice.

"Invite him over, honey-bunny. If he's a fairy it'll be nice to have him around. Just for kicks."

"Will you stop calling him honey-bunny," Derek said. "You know how he hates it."

"He does not hate it. Do you, Mr. Lazarus?"

Barney sighed impatiently.

Another parade was passing. Most of the musicians were drunk and had their hats on sideways. Whenever they could remember, the players blew loudly into their instruments or gave the drum a joyful thump. The bandleader and two trombonists had taken a wrong turn on the Calle San Vincente and had not been heard from since noon. A man of about forty years, tottering under his burden, supported a huge banner which proclaimed that his district's *falla* had won third prize in the civic competition. Behind the chaos of the band a more dignified group of about six or seven families marched proudly and in step.

Nearly every city block had undertaken to build a *falla*. The *fallas* were made of wood and *papier mâché* and, although they varied in size, almost all of them were satirical. Favourites, every year, were the ones which caricatured bullfighters and their managers. On each *falla* there were several figures filled with firecrackers. Every year the *falla* which won first prize was saved. All the others were burnt and exploded on the night of the *Día de San José*.

André looked away, over the crowds and into the square, at the tremendous *falla* standing in the plaza. The huge wooden figure of the plump gypsy, a thick, coloured scarf knotted around his belly and another scarf tied around his head, grinned dumbly back at him.

Barney tapped him meekly on the shoulder. He gestured wildly at his glass and pointed to his mouth. "YOU LIKEE DRINKEE?"

André looked up and laughed. His laugh was honestly hearty, joyful, and it sounded very good to Barney. André had been gloomy and he was pleased at the intrusion. "Me likee drinkee very much," he said, smiling affably.

"You're an American!"

"Canadian."

"That's just as good," Barney said.

"I guess so."

André felt slightly ridiculous. He hoped that Barney wasn't going to panegyrise the big and unpatrolled frontier. Or ask about Barbara Ann Scott, or if they resented the Governor-General.

"Wadiya know! A Canadian. My name is Barney Larkin."

Clutching to him insistently, Barney presented André Bennett to Jessie and Derek. Derek allowed him a perfunctory sneer, pretending ennui, but Jessie was favourably aroused, and she insisted that he sit down beside her.

Jessie patted down André's dry, brown hair affectionately. "Isn't he a doll? I bet he's a mountie and he's after his you-know-what." Her voice was silky.

Barney winked and slapped his hands up and down on his lap imitating a hoof beat. Derek winced and Barney's hopeful play faded quickly. Poor bastard, Derek thought, all he wants is to belong. But I haven't even got the humanity to grant him that.

The waiter arrived with the tray and Derek swallowed his cognac in one gulp. Immediately he felt giddy, daring, and he was worried about how he might act. He turned to André. "*Sabe Vd. hablar español?*"

"*Procuro cuanto puedo.* But I'm not very good at languages."

"You hear that, dear? He speaks Spanish."

Barney waggled his head happily.

"Are you a painter?" Jessie asked kindly.

"Of sorts."

"I'll bet he's damn good!" Barney said.

André looked at Jessie in a manner that was frankly appraising. Kinky, auburn hair, cut boyishly short, clung tightly to her head like soft sponge and tucked itself in neatly under her blouse collar. Her blouse was not actually transparent but the black brassière underneath was artfully present. Her lips were hard and badly disappointed. Her eyes were black and wet and frightened. Too much drink had deprived them of much of their natural intensity. She smiled at André. "How long have you been in Europe?" she asked.

"About two years, I guess."

"Your father sending you money?" Derek asked.

"No. I pick up jobs here and there. Chauffeur, translations, tours. Anything that comes up."

"That sounds very interesting," Barney said. "You and Derek ought to have a lot to talk about. He also lives in Europe. In fact Derek is something of an arti . . ."

"Something of a dilettante, that's what he means," Derek said savagely.

André said nothing. He had meant to visit Chaim that afternoon, but Chaim had warned him that he would be entertaining a special friend. I could be with Toni now, he thought. She must be in.

"What kind of painting do you do?" Jessie asked. "But don't get too technical now. I'm afraid I can't understand modern art."

"Who can?" Barney said, smiling good-naturedly.

"As a matter of fact," André said, "I'm not really a painter at all. I came here to study life in its entirety. One day I hope to write a book about it. You know, like that *Who Do the Bells Toll For*. I'm for calling a spade a spade. It's going to be an exposé of a coterie of lechers that hold hetero orgies in secluded Bloomsbury dungeons, and the hero is a guy who has just turned Red and written a book about his past activities as an anti-communist. One minute, perhaps I'll call it *Lost and Found*. Meanwhile I make ends meet peddling hashish at convent doors." Suddenly he turned to Derek. "Don't I know you? I'm sure I . . ."

"No."

"But I . . ."

"And don't be so facetious, *mon vieux*. We know what a burden it is to be intelligent."

"You talk as if you despised us," Jessie said. "Why, you don't even know us."

"I'm sorry. I was just trying to be smart."

Jessie smiled brightly. Underneath the table André felt her leg brush up against his own and stay there. "When are you coming back to America?" Jessie asked.

"I don't know. Maybe one of these days." All at once André felt very tired, and he wanted to get back to his room. "My family is very wealthy. I'm trying to make up for it."

Immediately André felt stupid. He had always been a failure at being bright.

"Now – is that funny?" Jessie asked.

"No. Not very."

"What outfit were you in during the war?"

A cigarette dangled from the corner of Derek's leering mouth. André noticed that he did not inhale. The cigarette was simply a device for striking dramatic airs.

"I was too young."

André felt more pressure on his leg. He wondered if it was just that she was drunk.

"You're a smart kid. If you ever get to New York," Barney said, "be sure and look me up. We can use bright young men like you in our outfit. After you get over this painter crap and all that, I mean."

"Thanks. It's something to think about," André said, grinning foolishly.

Another street urchin appeared and presented another dirty palm to Barney. He dug hastily into his pocket and pressed three pesetas into the boy's hand. "It's all a racket, André. But you've got to hand it to them. Take our hotel bill for instance. The damn thing is double because we come ..."

"Can't you ever stop thinking about money?" Jessie asked. Barney flushed angrily.

The sun was going down. The buildings seemed taller and fiercer and reached heavenwards pleadingly. The afternoon grin on the *falla* of the plump *Valenciano* had swollen into a diabolical leer. The clamour of a lost band shot through the air above the uproar of the crowds. Music came in waves. André looked at his watch and pretended to be amazed at the hour. "I really have to go now," he said. "Sorry. Thanks for the drink."

Jessie giggled. "You know why he brought me to Europe? I was sleeping with a boxer and he thinks if he shows me a good time I'll forget about it. Isn't that right, honey-bu . . . Oh, I forgot. Mr. Lazarus."

"She's drunk," Barney said.

"Where are you staying?" André hesitated. "I'll look you up later tonight."

"You're a liar!" Derek said.

André paused awkwardly.

Derek's face slipped badly. The unknown quality – that which gives unity and is called character – was absent. There was only the choking appeal in the eyes, the lips with a tendency to quiver, and the pain all over.

I could tell him, Derek thought. About Fox. About the mud. The songs. How the ammunition didn't fit and the guns jammed. "I'm not what you think. I – look, I fought here. I . . . Never mind. You wouldn't understand."

André felt the futility of the moment sorely.

"I know," he said suddenly. "Your name is Raymond."

"Yes."

"Then you wrote *The Edge*, didn't you?"

Derek averted his eyes. "That was a long time ago," he said.

Barney laughed uneasily. "Don't forget," he said. "At the Reina Victoria. We're staying at the Reina Victoria."

II

Chaim chewed on an unlit cigar.

Suddenly, his thoughts turned to André. It had been so long since they had had one of those endless talks. He hoped that André was in his room painting. I should have had him over this afternoon, he thought. I shouldn't have put him oV.

His mind began to wander again.

He thought about the Warsaw ghetto where those who were not burnt now walked the cold desert land, tugging at their beards, mourning murdered sons and murdered daughters, wondering if it was truly hot in the Promised Land. Chaim's teacher, Rab Moishe, had insisted that for two sins only did the common people perish. They spoke of the Holy Ark as a box and the synagogue as a resort for the ignorant vulgar.

Chaim plucked the wet cigar from his lips, uncorking his ever-handy bottle of muscatel. And after all, he thought, isn't it written in the Zohar that the pleasure of cohabitation is a religious one, giving joy also to the divine presence. He watched Carmen roll her nylons, which were part of his bribe of love, up her plump legs. How much butter and eggs go into the making of such glorious thighs, he thought? She caught his lewd grin and with a bound left the couch and settled down on his lap. But she failed to understand the disappointment in his eyes when her kiss was only friendly. "Carmen," he said, "really I wasn't so old once." He gazed at her with longing. "Now *vamos*. I'm expecting a visitor."

"I love you," Carmen said passionately.

"You're goddam right you do," Chaim said in English. "Me, and my cabaret, and my nylons. But it doesn't matter." Still his gaze lingered on her childish stupid face. He flung his pudgy hands up in the air in a gesture of lamentation. "What's going to happen to our *yiddish* children?" he asked.

There was a knock at the door. Carmen climbed clumsily off his lap, hugging him still. He waited until she had slipped into her skirt before he ushered Fräulein Kraus into the room.

He had been expecting this visit ever since Colonel Kraus had taken to loitering about the club. Now she sat before him, her quick blue eyes hard with contempt because she had been obliged to seek an appointment with her brother's employer, the Jew Chaim. Fräulein Kraus's hair was straight and fell in sharp lines from her face like a meticulously combed wig of string. Her face was bony and dry and tanned. Wrinkles were evident. Her body was thin, without sex, and the colour of old paper. She wore a short plaid skirt and a neat sweater. A pair of heavy woollen stockings were pulled up to her knotted knees.

Chaim spared Fräulein Kraus an introduction to Carmen. He nodded briefly when Carmen left the room. He felt as if Carmen and himself were part of a human conspiracy, and he enjoyed that thought.

"Well, Fräulein Kraus. Are you enjoying the *Fallas?*"

"No. Not very much."

"You would prefer the festival at Bayreuth? Or Munich?"

"You do not like Germans," she said, smiling coldly.

Chaim had a short, plump body. He was conscious of his dull physique so he preferred sitting to standing. His face was round and ordinary and his grey hair was thinning. Only his eyes illustrated the particular man. Liquid grey, profoundly expressive, they were the eyes of a melancholy clown, the eyes of a man who had absorbed so much of anguish that he was inclined to defend his human vulnerability behind a deprecating jest.

Chaim shrugged his shoulders. "Why should I dislike Germans? Bach, Beethoven, Mozart, Goethe – I could go on. Even Karl Marx was a . . ."

"Marx was a Jew."

They sat in his office above the Mocambo Club. The reflected light of the desk lamp glittered sternly on her steel-rimmed spectacles.

"Will you join me in a glass of muscatel?"

"I do not drink."

He refilled his own glass. First they must murder the human spirit, he thought. Stifle small selfishnesses, pleasures, then the organisation of inferior society might begin.

"We dislike each other, Herr Chaim," she said stiffly, "but . . . Spain is not my country and to be frank I find Valencia *dégoûtant*. Yet the Bolsheviks have made it quite impossible for a decent person to exist in my homeland today. I am a fascist." Fräulein Kraus paused. She felt it was necessary for Chaim to protest. But he said nothing, so she continued. "Don't think for a moment that I am prejudiced against you because you are a Jew. I respect a man for what he is. The only important thing in the world today is money. *Avec de l'argent même un juif peut épouser une comtesse française.*"

"Then you are a bit of a philosopher, Fräulein Kraus?"

Fräulein Kraus folded her hands in her lap. "You are making fun of me," she said.

Chaim lit his cigar. Yes. Fun, he thought. The fun will be for André and Toni's generation. They will have to pay the unpaid bills of the past, account for the dishonesties, the vagrancies, of Fräulein Kraus and myself. He switched off the desk lamp.

"You are fatigued, Herr Chaim," Fräulein Kraus said dryly. "Please, you must have come about something in particular."

Suddenly she realised that if Alfred still lived, had he not perished on the Malaga front, he would now be about the Jew's age, perhaps a trifle younger. "It is Colonel Kraus. My brother. He frequents your club often. I believe the fool is infatuated with one of the prostitutes in your employ."

Chaim felt spiteful. "Not the girl you just saw leaving my office," he said. "That would be most . . ."

"No." And to lay her tired ugly body down nightly, the taste of fifteen-year-old kisses still clinging to her lips moistly, ridiculing the pain of her unshared bed. "No," she said firmly. "Her name is Toni."

"But Toni is in love with somebody else. A Canadian. He is a very talented artist and a good man. They will soon be married."

"You do not understand. Colonel Kraus is infatuated with the girl. I think it would be wisest to forbid him entry to your club."

Chaim stood up. He circled the room, his pudgy, calloused hands clasped behind his back. "You hate him, don't you?" he asked.

"The Colonel? My brother?"

Chaim turned and looked at her. She sat unnaturally, almost off the chair – a wary hawk, he thought, unsafe, never trusting in the security of her perch. God, how she must have suffered!

"But you know how bright he is," she said. "What would he be if not for me?"

Chaim thought of saying "what is he?" but he knew what she would reply. He is a colonel. He was decorated by Hitler, and again by Mussolini. He was captain of the Olympic bobsled team.

Chaim conjured up a picture of Kraus. A man tall, awkward, and with an always troubled face, slow to comprehend but quick to violence. "I will not forbid him entry to the club," he said.

But she is probably right, he thought. I should warn André, for Toni's sake.

"If she is living with another man it would be best. Colonel Kraus can be difficult when he doesn't get his way."

"I'm sorry," Chaim said.

She got up. "There is something else," she said hesitantly. "You meet many people in your business. I was wondering. . . . You know I am a very well-educated woman. I won university prizes in psychology and I have published papers on . . . I have a doctor's degree. My favourite professor was a Jew.

I tried to help him when . . . As you know we are not prospering here. I . . ."

"So you would like to give lessons now. Perhaps you would like me to . . ." Chaim stopped short. Suddenly be felt an overwhelming compassion for her. He realised what it must have cost her in pride to ask a favour of a Jew. "Certainly, Fräulein Kraus," he said. "I'll see what I can do."

After she had left, Chaim walked over to the window. The streets were crowded: soon there would be another display of fireworks. The others are dead, she must go on living. Who am I to judge, he thought?

III

. . . as if in his sleep, long, untroubled, deep, he had made voyages to foreign lands, all of them hot and dry. In Xapolis of the Four Winds he had disembarked from his ship beneath the jutting crags that flanked the bay. Naked he had walked in the sun along the beaches of sands and shells, seeking the lovely Princess, Apoo, daughter of the great King Agramoo, so that he might ask of her that which sent him flying like a wild wounded bird up against so many distant shores. A question so far unanswered, so that he was prevented from winging homewards, windwards, across the big sky to his cave on the far side of the green green mountain, homewards where his faithful Aduku awaited him on the hearth rug admiring the pictures of many colours that he had painted on the rocks. And on the sands now, lovely Apoo walked towards him, flaxen hair filled with the Four Winds, herself naked except for the flowers circling her neck. And she said: I do not know but I think perhaps that you are guilty. Then I must go, he said sadly, and seek the Word of the Oracle of

Amkawa on another shore. So he set sail again, looking into the wind. . . .

The floor was a litter of paint-soiled rags, linseed drippings, brushes, paints, discarded sketches, and cigarette butts. A makeshift library was piled up underneath the window. A greasy kerosene burner and a coffee pot had been set up on top of the books. The pot had been stained many times by overflowing coffee so now it was almost all brown. Against the wall, in the corner, was a trunk that was used as a table. An overturned canvas served as a tablecloth. The cloth was strewn with breadcrumbs, pencils, two unwashed cups, an opened bottle of cognac, and a baited rat trap. There were two more rat traps on the floor. Several canvases – some unfinished, others untouched – were thrown up against the wall. An easel stood in the centre of the floor.

In contrast to this disorder the walls had been painted white. They were spotless, surgical, and blank. André had attended to this himself. For on first entering the room, one glance at the huge window facing northwards had satisfied him about the light.

Lying back on the bed now André reached drowsily to the floor for a wet brush. Selecting a particularly heavy one he flung it at the canvas that hung from the easel. *What drives us on*, he thought, *is the sense that we haven't tried everything. That perhaps somewhere there is God.*

In the morning he had begun his work in an orgy of enthusiasm. For two or three hours he had been certain that this was going to be his best picture yet. He had felt form and colour on his fingertips, just the way it had always been when he was painting right. And then, after a cup of coffee, he had decided that the flesh on the woman who lay dozing on the bed was lifeless. And he had begun to swear – swear, because he had wanted that if just anyone would touch that woman with a razor that the canvas would not tear but the flesh bleed. So he had gone back to work. . . .

It was bad, really bad.

André poured himself a cognac and flopped back on the bed. Just one is okay, he thought. I'm well now. He held up the glass before him, he enjoyed the warm gold colour. He thought: Ida is dead (I never loved her) and can't see colours. The cognac warmed his chest and he began to sweat. Ida is dead, he thought, and she cannot taste. He refilled the glass. I love you Toni, he thought. I love you so that you can destroy me. How long can it last? I love you and I am afraid.

There was a knock at the door.

"*Pase.*"

It was Pepe. He was one of the desk clerks at the Hotel Central. Their friendship dated back to the days when André had first moved into the hotel.

"Don't look at me like that," André said.

"You shouldn't be drinking."

"I'm all right now, Pepe."

"You were very ill."

And Pepe remembered how André had been afraid to sleep. And he, Pepe, would come up to his room and make coffee. They would sit there for hours, smoking under the hard yellow light, André not speaking but Pepe understanding he was not to leave him. And finally André would stop sweating and Pepe would go. How he used to call out her name in his sleep, Pepe remembered.

"You're so much fun when you're well," Pepe said. "The way you joke with María and make her laugh. Then you start to drink. Not that it was your fault anyway."

André grinned. He thought of telling Pepe about the man who had been following him but he changed his mind. He'll think that I'm being squeamish, André thought. He emptied the glass in the sink. "All right. I won't be morbid. I just like to hear you say it, that's all."

Pepe sat down on the trunk. He had a soft, big-featured face. His nose was too big and his black eyes showed all he thought. He had a trick of looking at you as if he didn't mean to forget – not what you said and not how you looked when you said it. It was nearly twelve o'clock. "Are you going to see Toni?" he asked.

Pepe didn't approve of Toni. At the bottom, he thought, she is a whore – *vale nada*. There will only be trouble. He is too sentimental about these things.

"Are you . . ."

"*Claro!*"

André began to strut about the room. It was always as if his body was new, and he was just going to try it out to see if it fit. He walked like an American – his long arms swinging loosely, his skinny legs taking big steps.

"Do you like my picture?"

Pepe got up and rolled himself a cigarette. He examined the picture carefully. "*Hombre*, what do I understand about art? Of course I like your picture. I like all your pictures because they make me feel good. Well, no. Sometimes they make me feel bad. But in a good way. Like the one you did of the crippled beggar, the green one."

André gave him a light. "How's María?" he asked.

"She wants you to have supper with us on Monday."

"Wonderful! But she might give birth any day now. I don't think . . ."

"She insists." Pepe scratched his head. "What are you looking for, André? Sometimes I think about it."

"I don't know."

"What do you mean you don't know?"

"I don't know."

Pepe shrugged his shoulders.

"It's something beautiful. Stalin isn't beautiful – he always wears a uniform," André said. "When I find it I'll know."

Pepe got up. "André. It isn't just that you're running away, is it?"

"No. At least I hope not."

"In your pictures you are running away. There is something missing."

"I know."

Pepe left.

André lay down on the bed and lit a cigarette. He remembered that time in Paris when he had decided that it, life, was a sardonic joke; and he had suffered from one of his worst migraines since childhood. Time had passed by aching inches and for purposes of simplicity he had divided it into the hours of light and the hours of dark. When he awakened it had always been too early for lunch or too late for breakfast. The burden of his migraine returned in full, he would get up and stroll along the *quais*. Then, he would return to his room and crawl back into bed. Sometimes he would watch the cockroaches slide slowly along the wall: other times he would try not to remember. Around seven he would get up again, eat, and go to a movie. Then he would return to his room and lie back in bed with his eyes open, unable to sleep. He always left the lights on because of the rats. Life had become a job for him, a mumbo jumbo with rules to be followed. Every night he would vow that he would not sleep in the next afternoon. But the next afternoon it was raining, or he was only going to lie down for a moment to digest his food. At night he would go to another movie. One night he saw three Technicolor Westerns.

If he tried to read a book he soon had to stop as he could not understand the meaning of the print. Once, to convince himself that he had not gone mad, he grabbed a pencil and wrote out the alphabet more than a hundred times. The hell with it, he thought. Never again.

IV

Madre mía!

Slowly María turned towards the other side of the bed, Pepe's side, towards the window and air and the pinpoint of light that shone from the lamp post, strong and like a star.

The pain, the stabbing pain in her lungs, had awakened her again. This time, anyway, she had managed an hour's sleep. The hollow sound of other people's laughter tinkled on the window pane like a rumour of happiness. She heard the noise of a car starting, again laughter, then the rising drone of the motor. She had been ill for two years now, but it always took her by surprise, the sharp pains that came so quickly. *Madre mía*, she gasped, *madre mía*. Again she rolled over in bed, slowly, so as not to aggravate the pain.

On the dresser, she could distinguish, among the other refuse, the doll her grandmother had sewn for her. But that was so long ago, years and years ago, further back even than the times of the picnics under the olive trees, further back even than the time she had refused to marry Alphonso because of the wart on his nose, further back even than the time of the American, the crazy, happy Negro who had pinched her that day. *If only it was true. If only she was going to have a child.*

She coughed – once, twice – and the quick pain came again.

Outside a drunk was singing.

> *Con bombas y con munición*
> *todos clases de gobiernos a destruir.*

The room was small. The flowery wallpaper had long since faded, and the damp disfiguring blotches on the wall were many years old. Several photos of pompous and ill-at-ease ancestors hung from the walls, all in heavy wooden frames. There was their wedding picture, and a crude landscape of which Pepe was particularly proud. Several drawings that

André had done of María were pinned up over the bed. An assortment of plates and cups (they had been part of María's trousseau) had been arranged on a wall shelf. And then a series of six plates had been nailed in a row down the wall, with slogans from Cervantes, Lope de Vega, and *El Poema del Cid*.

She heard the door creaking, opening.

Pepe sat down on the edge of the bed and kissed her.

Her health has improved, he thought. Her face is filling out, and her body also. But the doctor had said, Pepe remembered, that she must be kept warm and have plenty of fresh milk.

"Are you tired?" she asked.

Gently he leaned his head up against her swollen belly.

"Yes," he said. "A little."

"Do you think Luís enjoyed the supper?"

Luís, who had dined with them earlier in the evening, was an old comrade of Pepe's, from the days of the war.

"Of course he did. Why do you ask?"

"He should get married. He is too bitter."

"He is an anarchist. He doesn't believe in God," Pepe said.

"You shouldn't joke about such things."

Pepe grunted.

"You should pray sometimes."

Pepe grunted again.

"You are going to be a father. Your child will have to reckon with God."

"Reckon with God? For money a man may buy and sell God, let alone reckon with Him. God? What God? Can there be a God and He makes it a sin to be poor? Our shepherd! Is that what we fought and died in war for? So that superstitious women might taunt us with the lies of the clergy?" He stopped short. His own anger surprised him. "I'm sorry," he said tenderly. "I didn't mean to raise my voice."

"You talk sinfully!"

"Oh, María. Why do you believe such nonsense?"

"I believe, that's all. Does it hurt you?"

The pain came again. She trembled slightly.

"No. I'm sorry."

She fondled his head, running her fingers through his hair. From outside came the warming sound of men and women singing as they passed now and then in gangs below the window. Somebody had a *gaita*. He sang:

> *The miners of El Fondón*
> *We all wear berets*
> *With a legend that reads:*
> *"We have just finished at the mine."*

It was one of Pepe's favourite songs.

Pepe yawned. "André is working again."

"Pepe . . . ?"

"Yes?"

"What actually happened? Did he really kill the girl?"

"It's a long story. Very involved. He . . . just look at him!" Pepe said angrily. "Do you think he could kill?"

"No."

"Well?"

"Wasn't she a Jewess?"

"Let's not talk about it now."

Pepe sat up and rolled himself a cigarette. Dreamily he stared into the night. The magic of the *Fallas* reverberated within him. Only once had power been brandished before him. And now, like the others who were also hungry, he remembered – remembered because workers possessed the streets again, building wooden figures, shouting, dancing. "María! Our child will be a boy. We shall call him Jeem."

"If you wish."

"Remember? His Spanish was so funny. But that Jeem could play a harmonica. *Si hombre!* Seeing all that killing made him feel bad, he told me. He thought maybe if someone explained things to Franco, how the people really felt . . . What a crazy guy! Remember? Do you remember him, María?"

"I was very young," María said. "But I remember him."

"Do you, María? Honestly?"

"Yes."

"Remember how Jeem took the coffee from you and pinched your bottom with his big black hand? *Madre mía!* The way the men around the truck jumped back, everyone so frightened of your old mother. The bitch, she really did turn red in the face!"

"She was very angry," María said solemnly.

"Angry? *Hombre!* She yelled and waved her fat arms about as if the world was coming to an end. But Jeem just laughed and laughed. Remember how he grabbed her and began to rock her up and down in his arms as if she was a child?"

"He used to play good songs on the harmonica."

Pepe got up and looked out of the window. His face was in the dark and she could not see his black eyes that were wet and sorrowful with remembering. All she could see was his black curly hair, strong in the dim light.

"The harmonica seemed so important," Pepe said, sitting down on the bed again. "I got down on my hands and knees and began to search. I searched all over – in the truck, in the mud – but the harmonica had disappeared. I couldn't find it anywhere."

The pains came again, but she said nothing. She fondled his hair, humming an old song. Finally, she said: "I don't want it. Not for our boy. I want it to be different for him."

The Capronis, the Junkers, zooming and spinning over the slow dying city every night. In Alicante a visiting German destroyer had lit up the harbour for them.

"Why did he die, María? What did it mean?"

"I don't know."

"But you're religious. You believe these things happen for a reason."

A man was banging on a drum. The window pane rattled. My son is in her belly, Pepe thought, and it is warm and snug for him.

"It is not enough to say that he died for a cause. Nobody dies for a cause. They die for their women and their family. And he wanted to live for them," Pepe said.

She said nothing.

"Remember? He used to look so funny when he laughed."

"Maybe he died for you?"

He found her solemn face in the dark. Her deep black eyes were without expression and her lovely lips were quiet.

"For me?"

"So that you might understand something."

"What?"

"I don't know."

V

One a.m. or so. Ink, flat as a board, sky. Fog. Moon of the type in demand by sentimental virgins, i.e. pretty as a postcard moon, harvest moon, moon like from a story in *Good Housekeeping*. Dripping cold mist rolling up from the sea.

Hands thrust deeply in his pockets André jostled his way through the Plaza del Caudillo. He tossed himself headlong into the crowds, oblivious of rude comments, anxious only to lose himself in the mob. On the Calle San Fernando he stopped to buy a package of *tabaco rubio* from an old woman with a hare-lip. Tenderly she called him *señorito*, whistling the words between blackened teeth, and she tried to sell him a lighter. Remembering what Pepe had told him about these wretched women, how the *Guardia Civil* had their daughters in payment for sanctioning their illicit activities, he hurriedly bought a cheap lighter and moved on. He had walked only a few steps when he felt foolish, ashamed.

If anyone had asked him the hour – yesterday, now, tomorrow – he would have replied, ineluctably: "Five Minutes to the End."

   ... five minutes to when the mob plunging madly down the metro steps would be called to a halt, forced to stare into each other's eyes; five minutes to when the bankers and the priests of liedom would feel the finger of God hot on their backs, the irrevocable what's what finally demanded ... five minutes to when the squint-eyed clerks and the whores humpbacked by sin are told to bring their indifferent copulating to a stop ... five minutes until the blood-soaked rags that the swindled mob salutes and dies for are hauled down and burned ... five minutes to the big *l'addition, service non compris!* ... five minutes to when you and me, Jack, are gonna be told the score, like it or no – cheat and the boob strictly from hunger who's always been on the legit ... five minutes to when the lynched niggers and the charcoal *yids* and the rotting-green bodies of the betrayed soldiers get themselves another shot of juice and begin to roam this nogood nolovin world of shot ideas and neon depravity, demanding blood, revenge, no questions asked ... five minutes until J C returns with a new mob and new ideas, laughing his lovely head off, his boys selling gaga crosses with ads on the back in colours to match your rug. ...

In the old quarter behind the Plaza del Mercado, crumbling buildings of faded orange and sometimes sickly grey leaned lazily over towards the street. The yellow lights of night illuminated chalk slogans and obscenities that ran in streaks along the damp peeling walls. Discarded old men, lice creeping up their faces freely, snoozed in doorways.

   The stink of stale drainage and decaying fish clogged his nostrils. On the street corners the fat women doughnut vendors sat stirring boiling olive oil in huge cauldrons. He tried to destroy the visual image he still retained of the giant gypsy *falla* in the Plaza del Caudillo.

Two Worlds – Worlds, to neither of which he owed true allegiance – would collide and crush him. That, he often felt, made his doom inevitable.

Often it appeared to André that he belonged to the last generation of men. A generation not lost and not unfound but sought after zealously, sought after so that it might stand up and be counted, perjuring itself and humanity, sought after by the propagandists of a faltering revolution and the rear-guard of a dying civilisation. His intellectual leaders had proven either duds or counterfeits – standing up in the thirties to cheer the revolution hoarsely, and in the fifties sitting down again to write a shy, tinny, blushing yes to capitalistic democracy.

Nobody could quite believe again that he had grown up to find all Gods dead, all wars fought, all faiths in men shaken. There was going to be another war all right – their war. The Old Gods, newly cleaned and pressed, were being gleefully handled down by the generations that had made an orgy of self-destruction out of the twenties, and an abysmal flop out of the thirties, only to reap the bloody harvest of the forties. They, these prophets of the twenties, growing old without grace or wisdom or beauty; and the Public School revolutionaries of the thirties, plunging us gladly into another dark age rather than admit the fact of their poverty. All of them, screaming No, No, No! – we are guilty, all of us, because we were born you see and that's a sin.

This new post-war generation was born far too old for Mah Jong and ballyhoo and bathtub gin. The idea of the twenties they found charming and stupefying, a silly kink in our social history. They came to Paris again, but it was

different now. Only the fifty-year-old men-children, returning for maybe the first time since the twenties, attempted to
renew the calculated idiocy of their youth abroad, only they
boozed until six a.m. in Montmartre. This newer generation,
their children, gazed on the pathetic festivities wearily but
indulgently, sitting sad and unknowing in the cafés, sitting,
saying nothing and going nowhere, today being only the
inevitable disappointment of yesterday's tomorrow, waiting,
waiting for something they were at a loss to explain.

In his anxiety to keep on moving, not to see, he nearly stumbled over a crippled beggar. Both the man's legs had been
severed at the knees: a filthy cotton material was wound
around the stumps. He was sprawled out in the street singing
an imbecile tune, his skinny arms outstretched as if awaiting
crucifixion. Spread out before him in the grime was a weird
conglomeration of goods – tobacco, matches, flints, prophy-
lactics, crucifixes, and two tattered novels by Zane Grey. A
ragged dog was sniffing at the edge of his tiny universe of
wares. Quite suddenly the beggar gave him a swift wallop in
the ribs with a clenched fist. Then he began to cackle idioti-
cally, yellow spittle trickling down the sides of his mouth.
Several of the passing soldiers and whores joined in the
merriment. André followed the track of the dog as he raced
down the street amid a shower of kicks.

VI

During the war against Hitler heaps of Jews were murdered
and made into soap not nearly as good as Lifebuoy or lampshades much better than the crap they try to pass off as the
McCoy in department store bargain basements – it's not really

human skin at all now! But in the next war – some people say – the gang will find that commie skin really isn't as lampshady as the flesh off a kike's ass.

Chaim laughed at his own bad joke.

"I'm drunk," he mumbled aloud, not caring whether anyone in the crowded club overheard him.

After so many years in America perhaps it was the perpetual restlessness that was his weakness or perhaps it was simply a sad curiosity that drove Chaim back to Europe in the unfortunate spring of 1946. And then, of course, there had been the thin frightened boy, with a number and a symbol on his arm, who required a passport if he was to join Sarah in the Bronx. It had all been arranged, just as Chaim had promised. So in 1947 Chaim had crossed the Spanish frontier at Port Bou with a forged passport. He had remained in Barcelona for some time, living in a hotel in the Barrio Chino, first working as an interpreter and then as a smuggler. In the autumn of 1949 he had moved to Valencia and purchased the Mocambo Club on the Calle de Ruzafa, or the Calvo Sotelo as it was named after the War of Liberation.

"I'm drunk."

There are many strangers about, Chaim observed. Tourists in town for the *Fallas*.

But the regulars were also there – Maríano of the state police who believed there was a Freemason plot to overthrow the last of Catholic governments, Gómez who was sent over nightly by the Tango Club to spread rumours about the Mocambo dancers, Colonel Kraus who always arrived after twelve when his sister was asleep, Sasha who had been decorated by the Czar and now handed out perfumed cards for Casa Rosita, old Carlos who shivered rapturously whenever his Andalusian lover danced – the regulars; the cardboard men, the separated lovers, the broken republicans, the discards, all there, singing songs, embracing each other's skeletons in the endless search for warmth, begging emotional pennies.

Chaim walked around the bar towards Toni, but in passing Rosita he favoured her young bottom with a deft pinch. Rosita smiled agreeably. She hoped this vagrant intimacy might lead to greater things.

Chaim sat down beside Toni.

"I think I'm drunk," he said.

A florid waiter waddled over quickly to the bar and rattled off a series of orders to Ramón. He saw Chaim and turned to him pleadingly, his face flushed, his protuberant eyes red and darkly ringed underneath. He pulled out his handkerchief, mopped his brow and wagged his head meaningfully, once towards Chaim, once towards the crowd. "It is too much," he said. "I have changed my jacket three times in the last hour."

Chaim grunted. Then he turned to Toni. "*Shien maidele,*" he said, "where did you get the kitten?"

Smiling coyly Toni clutched a scrawny grey kitten to her breast. She tickled his belly with her finger and the kitten struck out playfully with his paws.

"I found him in the doorway."

She held out the kitten.

"*No importa!* I believe you."

Toni laughed and all her even white teeth showed.

Her hair was black, her eyes were lovely dark and limpid, her lips were always red and moist. She was a fisherman's daughter, from the island of Ibiza. The nobility of that island people, and their earthiness, was plainly on her face. Also grace, also indolence. She was small without being short and her body was strong and brown. Toni was beautiful, but it was the beauty of the young.

"Women always look so indecent when they're dressed," Chaim said.

"Do you think my sweater is too tight?"

"Don't try any of that stuff on me, *chica.*"

Chaim poured himself a glass of muscatel. He stood up and stretched his plump body with pleasure and a sense of sensual comedy. He felt for his stomach with his pudgy hands as if he found its presence reassuring. I'm not drunk after all, he thought. "Toni," he said, "*qué pasa?*"

"Guillermo is back."

"So?"

Toni set the kitten down on the bar.

"Nothing. I just thought I'd mention it."

"Does André know he's back?"

Toni looked away. The band was playing a shapeless tango without feeling. Putrifying puffs of smoke hung over the dancers. There was a lot of shouting and laughter. "Why don't they stop dancing? Why don't they stop?"

"Are you going to tell him?"

"No."

"But André and Guillermo are friends."

"Friends," Toni said. "Guillermo doesn't want friends, he needs enemies. And André . . . André is always alone." She pulled at the leather on the bar stool. "Even with me he is alone. He can get André into trouble. It is dangerous."

"That's André's business."

Toni brushed an imaginary bit of dust off her skirt. She bit her lip, and her eyes were wet.

"André is a child, Chaim. He has no skin. Only blood."

"No *chica*, that's not his problem. It is that he knows and understands all the things that he is against but he still doesn't know what he is for. André has the temperament of a priest but none of the present churches will do. That makes it very difficult."

"He wants to bleed for everybody."

Chaim dropped his hand on her knee and squeezed hard.

A spotlight was turned on the tiny dance floor. The couples on the floor, like an army dispersing, shuffled wearily back to their tables. They seemed to leave something of their sweat and something of their sorrow behind them, exposed under the hard and unwavering light. The lights around the club darkened and for an instant there was the illusion of coolness. Small bulbs under pink lampshades popped on on every table. They, the people, reached for each other's hands – clammy, unreassuring, and red under the lamplight.

"When a person is in a state of apprehension and cannot make out the cause of it (the star that presided at his birth and his genii know all about it), what should he do? Let him jump where he is standing four cubits, or let him repeat, 'Hear O Israel, etc.': or if the place be unfit for repetition of the scripture let him utter to himself, 'the goat at the butcher is fatter than me!' A Jewish joke, you understand?"

A drunken Frenchman in a dinner jacket stood up in one of the quasi-private booths that flanked the right wall of the club and began to applaud furiously. But the show wouldn't begin until all the tables had been replenished with drinks.

"Chaim, I'm pregnant."

"Well, that's not so bad. Does André know?"

"It's not his child."

Her eyes seemed very vulnerable in the dim light. We have different memories, Chaim thought; that makes this kind of talk difficult. He took a sip of muscatel.

"Chaim, I tried everything. I took pills. Hot baths every night. One night I jumped down the stairs three at a time. Another night I carried a heavy suitcase around until I fainted."

"Now don't get excited. It's not that serious. How long?"

Eulalia – lithe hips swaying under the spotlight, breasts very evident, muscular legs peeping through a slit gown – *España, no hay más que una,* and singing it very badly. The women in the audience sucked their lemon drinks, puffed languorously at their cigarettes, or eyed the man at the next table. The men, depending on their temperaments, followed the sway of Eulalia's hips or imagined the plenty of her breasts.

"Three months. It was before we began living together."

"That's not what I meant."

Eulalia bowed, her gown dipping slightly away from her, and the men applauded.

"I hate him! He forced himself on me. He used to pester me night after night. Finally, I . . . Well, I gave in, that's all."

She began to sob.

"You can tell him," Chaim said. "André will understand."

"He won't. You don't know him like I do. He thinks I'm naïve. Isn't that funny? In spite of everything he thinks I'm a child! He wants to protect me. Lovely Toni, he calls me. It would all be spoilt if he knew."

"Do you love him, *chica?*"

Toni tossed her head back sharply and laughed. Her long black hair fell back on the bar and the kitten struck out at it with his paws. She was trembling. "He could take me to America, Chaim. His family has money. I wouldn't have to live like this." She laughed again. "Don't you think his family would adore me? After all, how could they know?"

Chaim ordered Toni a cognac and waited silently until she had drunk it.

"Do you want to have an abortion?"

"Yes."

"What about the father?"

"He is far away," she said. "He . . . no, he isn't. But I don't want to have his child."

"Does he want it?"

"No."

The new quartet – *orgastic* trumpet, wailing saxophone, despairing piano, and neurotic drums – made an attempt at jazz. They had the beat wrong though, and it sounded quite forced.

"Tell André. He would want to know." Yes, I'm drunk, he thought. Now, I'm really drunk. "Tell André," he said.

Toni lit a cigarette. "What about the girl. Didn't she die of an abortion?"

Chaim shrugged his shoulders inscrutably.

"You won't tell me about it?"

"If he wants to he'll tell you."

The quartet was enthusiastically applauded. They had played an American song, and everybody applauded. Even the florid waiter stopped, and applauded. He thought: I have got a cousin in America. Roosevelt was an American, and he was a great man. The drunken Frenchman in the dinner jacket applauded. He thought: In America everybody is rich. Chaim didn't applaud because he knew the song, and the words, and it was badly played. Chaim said to himself:

> *Con-ju-ra-tion*
> *Is in his socks and shoes;*
> *Tomorrow he will have those*
> *Mean Sundown Blues!*

Toni got a handkerchief out of her bag and began to dab at her eyes. "You think I'm weak, *sinverguenza*. You think it has been dishonest of me not to have told him long ago," she said. "I never thought I'd meet a man like him. I'd do anything for him, Chaim. Only he mustn't think badly of me."

"You tell him about it, *chica*. If you decide to have an abortion I'll arrange it."

"Do you remember, Chaim? The first time I spoke to him it was here and he was drunk. He had been drinking for a week and I took him home. It was about four in the morning, and a lovely child was dancing in the street for small change. There must have been about five or six people watching her and André began to fight them. I couldn't stop him! He wanted to take her home with him, the fool! But the child was scared and she ran away."

Chaim motioned for Luís to bring Toni another cognac.

"Don't *chica*. Everything will be all right."

"I never told you what happened when I got him back to the hotel. His room, *madre mía!* The bed had been moved into the centre of the room and it was surrounded by a pile of books, suitcases, canvases, and bottles, built up as a dam. He said it was to protect him from the rats."

"*Tiere maidele*, he is neither a child nor a boor. You did more than anyone else to make him well."

Toni took a sip of cognac and coughed.

The spotlight was turned off. The bright lights went on again.

"Look," Toni said, "they are going to dance again."

"Yes, they are going to dance again."

"Do you think he'll want me to have the child?"

"Yes."

"It would always be between us."

"Not necessarily."

"I'm so afraid," she said.

Chaim stood up and kissed her on the forehead. "We'll have supper together tomorrow night, *chica*. Just you and me. The hell with André."

Toni embraced him. She felt relaxed and warm in his arms. She kissed him on the cheeks.

"Chaim, I'm afraid."

"Tell me," Chaim said, "just between the boys. Did you try hot gin?"

Toni laughed.

"Oh, yes, he's waiting for you at Ruzafa's. He was in earlier but he left again. He wanted to see the dancing."

VII

They began to assemble sober and even shy on the corners and plazas and alleyways shortly after midnight. Wooden bandstands had been erected on the street corners, and for a long time the jerky music of *pasodobles* swelled in the slums. Old men who had been searching the gutters for butts, pick-pockets, beggar children, plump mothers nursing bawling babes in their arms, pimps, ragged soldiers far away from home, aged cripples and the blind sellers of lottery tickets, unemployed workers and young girls – all the discarded junk and wonderful humanity of the slums joined hands for the dancing. Drunks tumbled out of *bodegas* to join in or at least harangue the womenfolk. The noise was tremendous, booming, wonderful, and crazy. Empty bottles crashed to the pavement, wineskins were flung up into the air. The shouting of one band soon got mixed up with another and nobody knew what kind of dance was being played. As long as there was noise, and shouting, and laughter.

Finally the whores showed themselves as well – dressed in sheer black gowns or form-fitting sweaters or slit skirts, drinking and joking and belching, just to show the wives how much they gave a damn. The gypsy boys appeared, cheap guitars slung over their shoulders, and they sat down on the kerb to play a *flamenco* or a *jota*.

"*It is very colourful,*" *Mrs. Ira Birks – visiting dignitary from the United States, wife of a Harvard Law School graduate, applecheeked, native of Little Oak, Conn., aged fifty-three, sexually incompatible with Mr. Birks, antivivisectionist, Vassar, class of '22, member – D.A.R., S.P.C.A., wrote poetry from 1920 to 1924 and still does the occasional watercolour, virginity lost in the back seat of a '19 Ford, favourite poet, John Keats – said, turning to Cardinal Megura y Paenz, Archbishop of Valencia.* "*I simply adore your fiesta! If only I weren't obliged to attend the bull-fights. . . .*"

The Ambassador laughed heartily.

The Archbishop smiled his thin and malodorous smile.

"Mrs. Birks is only joking," *the Ambassador said.*

They stood by one of the huge windows in the Exchange Building overlooking the Plaza del Mercado. The ball they were attending was in honour of the Fallera Mayor, *and the twenty-five piece orchestra was playing the Merry Widow waltz.*

Red-eyed drunk now, mad with the *flamenco* wail, the whores began to dance. Bleached blondes, jerking, twisting their bodies angrily; blackhaired bitches lifting their arms overhead and clapping desperately; old sluts shaking themselves into a frenzy and stamping their feet down on the pavement; giggling novices scream-singing until they soaked themselves in sweat. All for the dance, all for the song, all for the music.

Moaning guitarists, their hands ripping up and down the twanging strings and beating on the hard wood of their instruments, made with their magic joy or sorrow of the maddening mob.

> *Ai-aiii-ai-aii,*
> *Oooh aii yooii,*
> *En cárcel,*
> *En cárcel.*

"It is a good thing there is a strong hand over them," General Mellado – veteran of the Blue Division, son of a parish priest, first officer into Guernica – said. "Otherwise . . . No, I won't talk politics in the presence of such a beautiful and distinguished lady."

"Oh, but I adore politics, don't I, Henry?"

The Ambassador laughed heartily.

Sweaty hands clapping, swelling hands clapping. Voices upgoing, high, high. Soul music reeling on, on, on, tumbling, jerking, screaming:

Fuego! Fuego! Fuego!
Como huele a chamusquina!
Fuego! Fuego! Fuego!
Ay que no, que son sardina!

Bodies rattling with spiritpain, cavorting on the alive street. (A man grabs a woman and retreats into the shadows.) Eyes cravefilling, paining. (A girl bites the neck of her partner.) Mouths of disbelief and hunger, heads filling with blood and want. (A young girl swoons.) Veins of the neck swelling purplish, chests thumping and sweatful. (Pedro quells his quaking wife with a slap, and holds her to him.)

Fuego! Fuego! Fuego!
Mundos y planetas en revolución
con el fuego! De mi corazón!

"*What do you think of Graham Greene, Cardinal?*"
"*Greene . . . ?*"
"*Oh, it is nothing,*" the Ambassador said quickly, "*just a writer. Mrs. Birks is something of an intellectual. She often addresses clubs . . .*"

. . . and the guitarist slaps his guitar bang bang bang bang, and all is quiet. The buildings are quiet, the streets are quiet. So quiet, so still. Only the sound of breathing and only the stink of sweat. Even the clouds don't move, even God is wondering. (I shall walk up to heaven and turn off the stars one by one. I shall rub out the Milky Way with my heel and paint the moon in black. I shall kick the sun sizzling into the sea and I shall spit comets on all of Spain. If God is in I shall tell him why.) And the guitarist laughs. Laughs madly and like a devil. *Dinero*, he says, *dinero*. A crippled child moves among the crowd, collecting *centimos*. The people rest and drink.

"*Oh, but they dance divinely!*"

The General laughed jovially. "Men will be men."
Mrs. Birks smiled.
The Ambassador laughed heartily.
"God bless them," said the Archbishop.

They danced until their bodies ached from excess of pleasure (and they thought the earth had fallen out of the sky), they danced until their eyes were swollen with need of sleep (and they saw the buildings were of gold and the streets of soft silk and the lamp posts lit by glowing diamonds), they danced until they were too drunk to stand (and they believed the sun was hot and the earth was friendly and the grass was green in spring), they danced until Sunday's dawn filled the sky gloomily and without promise (and they believed in the day and God and they were no longer afraid).

VIII

Kraus was not drinking. He was seated alone at the bar, his eyes fixed and brooding. He seemed to be pursuing a memory which had evaded him in the past, and which – considering his expression – he knew would evade him always. Chaim sat down beside him. He had had a lot to drink and he was feeling belligerent. "Roger," he said, "are you in love with Toni?"

Kraus grinned insipidly. But Chaim had startled him. "I don't understand what you mean," he said.

"You have been following André."

Kraus frowned. Until now following André had lacked excitement, but since Chaim was so concerned perhaps he had not wasted his time after all. Only that afternoon Kraus had tried to make out what André was saying to the Americans, but they had been speaking too quickly for him to understand. "I don't know what you are talking about," he said.

Chaim gripped Kraus by the arm. His face was flushed. It was the first time Kraus had ever seen him angry. "Roger, I have never threatened you," he said, "but I'm warning you now. Do you know how easy it would be for me to have you carried off to France? Do you know what it would mean if they found you in Toulouse?"

Kraus laughed cockily. "You wouldn't," he said. "Theresa says you haven't the courage."

Chaim let go of his arm. "Don't you understand? Theresa despises you."

Kraus got up. A waiter came between them and he pushed him out of the way. His face was drained of colour. His eyes were hard and vacant. "I know about your passport," he said. "If I was making threats I should remember that."

Chaim lit his cigar. It serves me right for making threats, he thought. "Why are you following him?" he asked wearily.

"I'm going."

Chaim stood in his way.

Kraus seemed unsettled. "I don't know why. I'm not . . . Theresa says he is . . . He fascinates me." He stopped. "I'm human too, you know. It was only a war. Why shouldn't I have a girl as well?"

He looked at Chaim as if he was startled by what he had told him. He pushed him out of the way and hurried towards the door.

Chaim turned to Luís. Luís poured him a glass of muscatel. His eyes were burning. "If you need me or the others, Chaim," he said, "all you have to do is say so."

Chaim looked up sharply. "Tough guys," he said. "The world is full of tough guys."

Luís looked away. He began to wash glasses.

IX

André noticed her just as she started across the street – her hips pushing against her gay print skirt, her breasts very nice in her summery blouse, her legs quick, and taking small steps patiently. She paused to let a taxi go by. She curled her lower lip fretfully, so that now she was not only lovely but wicked-looking also. André suddenly felt clumsy, restless also, the way he always did until she sat down beside him. Nice, grace-ful Toni, he thought.

"*Querido!*" she said, as if it was a wonderful surprise to find him waiting for her.

"Hullo, yourself," he said shyly. "Sit down."

"I looked for you," she said.

"I know."

"Why didn't you call today?"

"I was on my way up to your place this afternoon, but I ran into some Americans."

"I'm so tired, *guapo*. My feet are stinging like many bee bites: I have danced with so many clumsy brutes tonight. Please buy me a cognac."

André called the waiter and ordered two cognacs.

"Tell me a funny story," she said.

"I don't know any."

"Then make one up."

"Toni, please!"

"Act your age, Toni," she said, mimicking his hard baritone.

He laughed uneasily. He felt she was forcing herself and he wondered what was wrong.

"Let's do something silly tonight," she said.

"Like what?"

"I don't know. Just something. Anything. As long as it isn't ugly. I can't . . . André! Guillermo is back. He came by tonight asking for you. I told him I didn't know where you were."

André said nothing.

"The police are looking for him. I don't want you doing any drawings for him or giving him money. It's not as if you were a communist."

"*Maldito!* How could you tell him you didn't know where I was?"

Guillermo was a small, agile man. The last time they had met, it was months now, had been in Cosmi's Bar. Guillermo no longer wrote lovely sonnets celebrating love. "*This is not the time, camarada. Now we must hate. It must be our religion.*"

"Please don't see him."

"Where is he?"

"He's coming up to my room tomorrow. André, please!"

André ran his hand through his hair and began to scratch nervously. He looked at her, his eyes slow and deepening, and she despised him for it. It was all right when he was angry or drunk, but when he turned inwards and faraway she lost all patience – it was unfair, unkind, for if they were lovers they should share everything.

"Do you still want to do something silly?" he asked tenderly. She didn't answer.

"We could yank Chaim out of bed and make him come swimming with us?"

"Don't make concessions for me, André! I know what you are thinking!" Now all her gestures were quick, and she spit out her words. "You are thinking she is a woman and she doesn't know about these things. But you are children! Ho, you and Guillermo are going to change things! Yes, you are revolutionaries. Sure, 'we would rather die on our feet than live on our knees.' So my father – also a fine revolutionary – is dead. My brother is dead. My uncles are dead. And for wh . . ."

"Toni, I . . ."

"No, let me finish! You and Guillermo have discovered that there is poverty and injustice, you . . . pooh! There has always been poverty. You can do nothing, do you understand?

Nothing! Why? What is the use of talking? Kill, and kill, and kill. Me, I would rather live on my knees. Now, I have said it!"

She was breathing quickly and that made her breasts prominent. He remembered them naked, lovely, soft like no other thing soft, and he wanted very much to lay his head on her breasts now, perhaps dragging on a cigarette, but slowly, easily, and she would stroke his hair, and she would say: "It is all right. It is all right."

"I can think of nothing to say except that he is my friend."

"That is no answer!"

"You are angry with me."

"That also is no answer."

I want only the clean things, she thought. I have had enough of the rest. "Love me, André," she said.

He grinned, but impatiently.

"Love," he thought. That is one of the words that is no longer any good. Like *courage, soul, beautiful, honour*, and so many others. Words that have become almost obscene because of the whoring of the hack writers.

She dropped her hand on his knee. Even his body was tight, she could feel such things. Already he is thinking about him, she thought. About what they will talk about. "All he had to do," she said, "was to go down on his knees and cry, '*Viva Franco!*' It was such a little thing! But he said no, never. The man who shot him was from Florence and he had studied for the priesthood."

"They would have shot him anyway, Toni."

"Perhaps."

"Drink your cognac."

"In the summer they would take us out in the boats and we would jump overboard and swim. The water was very cool, and there was always the taste of salt in our mouths. The priests said it was evil because we all swam and played together and we were often naked. My father laughed at the priests, he said they had filthy minds. At night there was always dancing on the quays, especially when there was a good catch. That night there was only the noise of the shooting." Suddenly Toni laughed a quickly joyful laugh and her eyes were glad. "Are we going to make love tonight, *guapo?*"

"You want to come to Canada with me, don't you?"

"Yes."

"Why, yes?"

"Because it is good in Canada and there is lots of money, and girls like myself don't have to work in cabarets."

"How do you know?"

"Everybody knows."

"And what would we do in Canada?"

"You would paint great pictures. We would have a big family, and at night we would go for a drive in your father's car."

His shoulders slumped. "How do you know my father has a car?"

"Hasn't he?"

"Yes. But he wouldn't lend it to us. He isn't sure that I'm his son. He thinks I might be the son of a guy named Serge."

"Serge? Tell me about Serge."

"Not now."

"Yes. Now!"

André lit a cigarette. The street was empty. He blew a big puff of smoke into the damp night air and smiled tenderly at Toni. "Crazy, lovely Toni," he said softly.

"*Ahora!*"

"Serge was one of my mother's lovers. He was a kind of poet, I guess. They edited a magazine together. She was madly in love with him. Serge, on the other hand, adored me and my mother's Cadillac. I was young. I understood nothing about those things. Finally, mama gave him up for a painter.

"Although poor Serge suspected that he was altogether incapable, my parents believed that I was his son. My father because from the very beginning I was 'unbalanced' and rebellious and 'gifted,' my mother because it all would have been so utterly romantic. But none of it is true."

"You are very ugly when you tell me these things."

An old, stooping man made his way down the street picking up cigarette butts from the gutter. He found a piece of bread and bit into it.

Toni pinched the inside of his thigh. "Would you like me to have babies for you?" she asked.

"No."

"Big, strong, Spanish babies."

"No."

"*Hijo de puta!* Why, no?"

"Let's go," he said.

"Okay, honey," she said in English, pretending that she was chewing gum.

Coward, he thought.

They walked along slowly.

"Recite a poem for me, *guapo*."

"I can only recite English poems, *favorita*."

"I don't care about the meaning. I like the sounds of the words. English words are so hard. You always look so serious when you recite. You make me laugh."

"So I make you laugh, eh?"

"*Si señor*."

They were on the Calle de Colón, not far from the gardens.

"Where are we going?"

"To the river."

Always, he wanted to go down the river. Why did it fascinate him so? But she made no objection. She pushed him into a doorway and held him and kissed his lips and throat. She tickled his ribs playfully. Then she kissed him again, nipping at his ear. "You are not going to think about Guillermo. You are not going to be sad. If you are sad I'll kick you where it hurts."

He embraced her warmly.

They passed several *fallas* on their way down to the river, each one posturing like a predatory ogre in the darkness. The light of the lamp posts pasted a glistening sheen on the backs of the wooden structures, suggesting a sort of supernatural sweat. As far as he was concerned their construction hadn't sprung from the spontaneous mischief of a fiesta-minded city but instead was part of the master plan of some diabolical spirit. As if they were not going to be burned, but had to be burned.

"Miguel was in tonight," she said. "He is such a sweet boy, *muy simpático*. His parents are very strict, you know. It was his first time in a cabaret. He told me that he had dreamt about me and in his dream he owed me two hundred pesetas. All the time he was talking he was blushing like a girl. I told him he had dreamt about Carmen, and that she was very pretty and would be overjoyed to get her two hundred pesetas. He understood. I introduced him to Carmen."

She glanced at him coquettishly, anticipating an amusing remark. His face showed nothing.

I will not tell him now, she thought. It is not a good time.

Suddenly André stopped short. "Somebody as lovely as you! How in God's name can you be a whore, Toni?"

"*Guapo* is excited and saying cruel things."

"What do you think of when you're in bed with a strange man? Do you say your beads?"

"Stop! Don't talk like that."

"I once made love to a slut in Barcelona and she crossed herself before she got into bed with me."

"André!"

He grabbed her. He kissed her longingly, holding her hard against him. "Don't pay any attention, Toni. Not when I talk badly. I . . ."

She leaned her head on his shoulder. He felt her nails digging into him. "I'm not a whore. I don't sleep with strange

men. I only dance with them. You know that. It's the only job
I can . . ."

"Please, darling. Don't. I must be crazy to say such things."

He lit a cigarette and gave her a puff.

Before them loomed the landscape of the Rio Turia. A
belly of yellow weeds and burnt grass, anæmic sands and
stones, trickling mosquito-ridden streams. O Turia! O tur-
bulent river! How you had once been proud! Overflowing
mighty banks, heaving chaos and destruction on the city.
Drowsy workers had eaten of their noonday bread whilst
dangling their legs over your banks. Children had swum,
sometimes drowning, in your powerful currents. And the
swollen barges, heaped up with oranges and figs and grapes,
rolling down your pitching waters. Roman soldiers had
stopped here to wet their heads, the voice of Seneca boomed
across your banks, the Cid of whom all Spain sings knelt here
to pray, and James the Conqueror, on his way to liberate the
city, paused on this spot to water his majestic charger. Here
the Knight of the Sad Countenance had sworn his fidelity
to the incomparable Dulcinea while weary Sancho dreamed
of his governorship under an olive tree. More recently still,
German shells belching news of the modern world into the
city, had dropped, momentarily sizzling, in your waters. . . .
How many suicides? What did it matter whether they were
Falangists or Reds when their young bodies toppled into currents swelling with the blood of revolution?

And now, opulent Turia, where is your glory?

Starving workers, bellies bloated big with grief, farm
splotches of your desiccated bed. Dead, debauched giant!
Rendezvous for pauper lovers! Unemployed newlyweds beget
dead children in the niches and apertures at the bottom of your
concrete sidings, lost men cook dead rats over twig fires, talk of
life and death and revolution, finally crawling into the damp
dark caves to huddle against the cold of night. . . . Are these the

men who write *Arriba España! Siempre Franco!* in a neat unhurried script on the concrete walls? Are the dogs who paint the slogans the ones who career crazily over towards the bridge when a butt is tossed out of the window of a speeding car?

Walking down the concrete steps hand in hand they were both immediately aware of the stink of stale human excrement and damp urine. They held their breath until they had walked out on the river bed.

Toni knelt down, peering into a tiny stream of stagnant water that weaved its way snakily in and out of a sandbank. The pool swarmed with mosquitos and squeaking frogs. It exhilarated her somehow, this tiny stream. She looked up. He seemed distant.

"Tell me something about America," she said.

It was no longer dark. The sky was grey. Pulpy clouds lifted themselves up by a faint violet glow that clung to their bottoms. He stood rigidly upright, pretending he was of the big sky, no longer of the earth.

I have a right to forget, he thought. I love her. We are young. The world owes the young certain rights.

"The sky isn't like this in America," he said. "It is like a prison roof painted blue. Here, it's different. Unfinished, like a Goya. There's always something more important than anything in it. But it's missing."

"Do you think your mother would like me?"

"She never likes anyone I like. Especially a woman."

Slowly the violet hue was swallowing up the clouds. The big eastern sky was full of burning orange and pink lights. Climbing, slowly climbing higher. The pallid disc of a white moon was fading away, dissolving into a copper mist dimly.

She had captured a frog. Clutching it in her tiny fists she pushed it under his nose. Suddenly the frog, its quick legs outspread, leaped out of her hand and bounded across the air into the stream, making a plop as it hit the water.

She turned to him. "Oh, I'm so happy, darling. How beautiful to be in the country!" Quickly she slapped him on the tail of his jacket and ran off. "Catch me, André. Come on!"

Sadly he watched her run off, over the muddy bed and across the splotches of dry grass. Suddenly he was afraid.

He noticed that a tall man was standing on the bridge and watching them. It was the same man who had been following him for the last week or so. When André looked up the man turned away.

He hurried off after her. "Toni! Toni!"

A hundred yards off she had fallen down giggling, rolling over on a patch of grass. He tumbled down beside her and grasped her firmly in his arms. "Toni, I love you."

He had never said it before. Not even to Ida. Now he felt ashamed and silly. It was such a cliché! Toni, I love you.

She kissed him passionately, crushing herself against him.

And she felt fear because she loved him with a hopeless beautiful love, knowing, always knowing, that he could not love, that something ugly and bitter within him would always stifle any love he felt for her.

"What is it?" he asked.

"You are going to die."

"What? What, my darling?"

She kissed him again.

"What?"

"Nothing."

"Yes, but . . ."

She embraced him tightly, urgently, pulling his head down to her lips. "Nothing, my darling. Nothing."

Book Two

SUNDAY

Men frequently think that the evils in the world are more numerous than the good things; many sayings and songs of nations dwell on this idea. They say that a good thing is found only exceptionally, whilst evil things are numerous and lasting. Not only common people make this mistake, but many who believe they are wise. Al-Razi wrote a well-known book *On Metaphysics* (or Theology). Among other mad and foolish things, it contains also the idea, discovered by him, that there exists more evil than good. For if the happiness of man and his pleasure in the times of prosperity be compared with the mishaps that befall him – such as grief, acute pain, defects, paralysis of the limbs, fears, anxieties, and troubles – it would seem as if the existence of man is a punishment and a great evil for him.

MOSES MAIMONIDES

I

MADAME! CONSIDER for a moment the world at large. Coming up sun filling in the empty sky. A just so-so morning (really). Greenwich reports the stars of last night succumbed in an ordinary way. Ditto the moon. It will be, by all reports, an ordinary day. As per usual people sleep. (Some snoring, some not.) In Pittsburgh, U.S.A., Mr. Peter Kalowski, who in twenty-seven years of service with Ajax Dairies, Inc., has never been late for work, creeps out of bed for his breakfast at three a.m. In the kitchen he notices that Mrs. Kalowski has forgotten to prepare his sandwiches. He takes the carving knife down from the wall. He re-enters the bedroom and stabs fat Mrs. Kalowski to death. (Tomorrow in court he will plead temporary sanity and get off with 199 years to life.) In Dwing, Herts, the outraged (Minister) George Barrin, writes (to be mailed to *The Daily Express* at nine a.m.):

Walter Jacks deserves suspension for putting a Sunday dinner before worship of God (*Daily Express*, April 8) and encouraging others to do the same.

There is no need to miss one's dinner. For years I have had the pleasure of my wife's company in the House of

God on Sunday morning and still had a hot, well-cooked dinner at 12:30.

Foresight and a regulated cooker helps a lot.

Regardless of the revolution and the absence of American recognition Mr. Ching-Tsu lies on the floor of his straw hut in Ping-Ling rattling with death in a scientifically approved manner. Mrs. Ching-Tsu, a rice-bowl Christian, kneels on the straw, praying to an unlistening crucifix of a slant-eyed Christ hanging from the wall. (Nearby, Reilly, the missionary, sleeps. A chink, he thinks, is something to convert, like the red injuns was.) In New York, Local 231 of the Toy Makers Union is working overtime to meet the big demand for atomic hats ($3.95 per doz/whsl) for the over-privileged kiddies of American damnocracy. (You, Bershenko of Kiev, that sore in the back of your throat wasn't concocted on Wall St. It's cancer, comrade.)

It is now 11:30 a.m., Sunday, April 18, 1951.

Valencia, Spain.

On the corner of the Calle San Fernando a man is playing a guitar and singing. His fingers are spilling, splashing, over the strings.

> *Manolete, Manolete,*
> *El mejor matador de España.*

But Roger Kraus – favouring his left leg which was broken in two places in the wrestling matches in Berlin and carrying two ounces of lead slug that hit him with an unforgettable impact at Cuatro Caminos in November, 1937 – hears (staring ahead of him and into nothing), and does not hear, hears and remembers other songs. Remembers:

> *Die Fahne hoch,*
> *Die Reihen fest geschlossen,*

> *S.A. marschiert*
> *Mit ruhig festem Schritt.*
> *Kameraden, die Rot Front und Reaktion erschossen,*
> *Marschiern im Geist*
> *In unsern Reihen mit.*

remembers,

> *Deutschland, Deutschland, über alles,*
> *Über alles in der Welt,*
> *Wenn es stets zu Schutz und Trutze*
> *Brüderlich zusammenhält.*

and remembers Alfred's song,

> *Die Heimat ist weit*
> *Doch wir sind bereit*
> *Wir kämpfen und siegen für dich*
> *Freiheit!*

For he, Roger Kraus, had been present with 5,599 others in the Zirkus Krone, Munich, on that historic and grey and rainfilled night of February 8, 1921, when after the ineffectual Drexler had spoken, the angry man in the brown trenchcoat gesticulating wildly, his voice hysterical, his grammar bad, had told 5,600 souls the truth about the "International Jewish Stock Exchange Parties" and about "Future or Ruin." So Roger Kraus – failure as a student, dreamer of yearning dreams and wanting badly to wanton, born October 8, 1899, into a family of minor officials, veteran, inarticulate, in love with his sister who despised him for his stupidity and was having an affair with a communist, discharged from three jobs, the last (in a Jew bank) because he had startled Fräulein Freida, poor, hungry, ridiculed all through gymnasium by rimless-glasses Jew intellectuals, Aryan, confused, sometimes following girls home at night – found (February 3, 1921, Munich) that he too had a place and a time and a card to show that he was a member.

Roger Kraus served the N.S.D.A.P. well. As an athlete, and as a soldier.

In 1935 he was sent to Spain. Here he was an intimate of *Hoheitsträger* Hans Hellermann and frequently appeared on Fichte League platforms. Officially employed by Hellermann & Phillippi as a member of the Harbour Police, he worked as an informer and a hunter of men, taking orders from Carl Cords and occasionally from Zuchristian. In Madrid, during July, 1936, he distributed Mausers or early potatoes to Lafarga and Torres. Later in the year he joined Queipo de Llano's army. In 1938 he was decorated for exceptional service by Generalissimo Francisco Franco.

Kraus, under sentence of death in Paris, returned to Spain in 1945.

He disliked Spain. The men were effeminate, Semitic, and they made poor soldiers. Even when they killed it was always from a passion, never with a sense of order. But these were bad times and he must be satisfied with anything.

He examined his reflection in the hallway mirror. The clothes are bad, he thought. They hang loosely from my body. She should see me in my uniform. My boots black and polished, my legs masculine, slender, my tunic tight against my chest. Still, I have the figure of a young man. My muscles are hard.

Not like Chaim – soft: plump: Jew. Godless.

And Chaim reminded him of last night. Theresa had quarrelled with him again, and Toni had avoided him at the Mocambo. So he had gone on to Noël's and there, young Chicu, drunken again, had greeted him with a mocking "*Sieg Heil*, Colonel." There had been others in the bar but Kraus knew them and that they were cowards. He had grabbed Chicu and swung him around so that his arm was pinned in back of him. Then, gradually increasing pressure on his arm,

Roger had ordered him to lay his other hand flat on the bar. He had drained his beer mug while Chicu crouched, whimpering, his hand quivering on the bar. Then, quickly, swiftly, he had smashed his beer mug down on Chicu's hand. He had heard the bones crack, and he had felt Chicu go limp and fall to the floor.

Godless, he thought. Impudent, and cowards.

But street brawls. . . .

Yes, the last months had been bad. He, Roger Kraus, was a soldier. But there were no calls. He was without an army or a commander or a reason. There had to be a reason, a prey, an enemy. Not this nothing, this waiting, this freedom.

She will be surprised to see me, he thought.

And in his room André puffed solemnly at a cigarette. The light was not strong enough for painting but it was sufficient just now to stare down at the street with nothing to do but think or wonder.

So many souls arising and greeting the new dawn dull-mindedly. Chaim, what is old Chaim thinking? (You are wonderfully wrong, old Chaim – *We cannot love all men because many of them are evil and not worth the cheapest of our sentiments which is pity.*) In Montreal, mother is awakening and father is yawning (eyes half-shut because he doesn't want to see mother's wrinkled body), and with the ineffable confidence of the untried he stretches and decides he will wear his trousers with the grey stripe. . . . Pepe is stirring, perhaps María is ill, poor Derek is probably staring into a mirror.

But me, what do I believe in? Not even in the validity of my own anger. (We, doomingly haunting a back-alley of pre-history, suffer the asking warlords and gods unworthy of men.) *But is it necessary to believe in something?*

Because I do not know enough or cannot guess enough or feel enough I believe in being good and understanding and brother to other men and painting because it is the only thing

I can do half-well and perhaps finally it will explain to me what I am looking for.

As a child, and later as an adolescent, André enjoyed wandering on the mountain which rose like a camel's hump in the heart of Montreal.

He had been brought up in Westmount where the Canadian rich lived, and every morning at eight his father got up and had breakfast and had Morton bring around the car and drove down to St. James Street where the Canadian rich worked.

André had attended a private school, and in the morning old pinhead Cox forced all the students to take cold showers. He studied Latin and in sixth grade got caught with a copy of *Sunbathing* in his desk and he made left-wing on the school hockey team. At night his mother read him the poems of Bliss Carman and his father dozed or approved of the editorials in the *Gazette* or recited a poem by Rudyard Kipling. His mother had many lovers and named him André because his father wanted to call him George after the King. André adored one of his mother's lovers, Jean-Paul, who did not last too long. Jean-Paul stole things, he called André's father *le roi des yahoos* to his face and his mother *la belle Lucretia* which André did not understand until later on, he was perpetually drunk and borrowing money and he was killed when a training 'plane he was in crashed during the first months of the war.

Yes, one fine day you got up and it was war. (It was not war when Guernica happened and the woman said *vale más morir de pies que vivir de rodillas*. No, not yet. But now Mr. Chamberlain said I am speaking to you from number 10 Downing Street and Mr. Hitler said up Germans and the *Montreal Gazette* said Save Your Scrap Iron.) So Mr. Bennett got up in the Mount Stephen Club and said gentlemen, this is war: he came home and he told André how it makes a man out of you: Mrs. Bennett knitted socks for the Red

Army: and every week André made a bundle of the *Gazette*s and drove down to salvage campaign headquarters with Morton.

But what did it mean?

As a boy living in it the war had meant The Walls Have Ears, hurrah for Churchill, Send us More Japs, V for Victory, up the Yids, Open up a Second Front, send your laundry to the chink, Buy Bonds, bravo the red heroes, Hitler has only got one ball and Goering has none at all, United Nations with Flags Unfurled, hip-hip the frog maquis, and so on. But later, just one year ago, he had visited a beach in Normandy. There were craters in the gravel; and he had found a black boot with a bullet hole in it. Pillboxes, at least four feet thick and crazy-coloured, lay smashed on the surf like the toys of giant children. The town itself, Ste. Famille, was abandoned and a ruin. So all through the night he sat up on the beach and tried hard and with no success to see the men charging out of the sea and falling with bullets in their bellies, and feel the Germans warm in their pillboxes firing away and muttering ach, swine – but men didn't do that kind of stuff or he was crazy or freezing and Judy came out at dawn and found him with the boot in his hand and trembling and he slept like a baby in the car all the way back to Paris and he was drunk for two days and the gang said he was being dramatic. . . .

So he came to Spain, Valencia, where the killing had started in a way and maybe they could explain it.

Yes, there were truths.

The Communists had one and so did the Christians. Even the bourgeois had one and for a long time they did pretty good with it. But you could not paint, not really, so long as men were killing each other so often. There was *the* truth, a shining beauty of a truth, and if he was strong enough he would find it. But until then, until that never day, his centre would be confusion. He would accept what came and act or choose according to what he knew, for not to act would mean non-living, which was the lot of the coward.

Toni's room was small and simply furnished. There was a discoloured yellow square on the wall where in 1937 a portrait of *La Pasionaria* had hung. In 1943 a student had committed suicide in the room by slashing his wrists. The blood had been washed away but where the pool had dried the floor varnish was still rubbed out. Then, for some time, the building had been run as a brothel. When Señor Jorge purchased the establishment only a year ago and had converted it back into a rooming house all the mattresses had had to be aired. The cracked springs were never mended.

I know better than he does what he wants, she thought. For one thing this is not his home and the sadness of Europe is wrong for him. So is politics, Guillermo, and Pepe. His anger against his family and his country comes of love and later on we will go to his land. A man should have a home and a family for without it he is a tramp. We will have a fine home in the mountains. He shall have a room full of books, and I shall sew for our children in the parlour. We shall be happy and have many quarrels. When we die our children shall carry on.

But the new will be strange. Perhaps the people won't like me?

André had left early. Last night he had been particularly restless in his sleep and twice Toni had had to get up to cover him. He had left a note.

Darling,
    You looked so lovely asleep I didn't dare wake you.

                             A.

    Send Guillermo around to my room as soon as he shows up.

She was in her dressing-gown, moving drowsily about the room, when she heard the knock on the door.

"*Pase.*"

Kraus entered the room and Toni shivered. Oh, my God, she thought. What if he saw him? What if they met in the hall?

Kraus smiled secretively, trying to affect superiority.

"You mustn't come here," Toni said.

The room is full of sleeping smells, she thought. *Our* smells. She walked over to the window and opened it.

"Why?"

Toni wrapped her gown more closely around her body. Underneath she was naked and she felt he knew. She felt nauseous.

"Why mustn't I come here."

"You mustn't," Toni said. "I forbid it."

Kraus sat down on the bed. It was still warm and unmade. She was not alone last night, he thought.

"Why?"

"Please, go. Please."

Kraus felt uneasy. With men – real men – his exploits were sufficient proofs of his power. But although women were reduced to a groaning and passionate avowal of his manhood in bed they resented and even mocked him in the morning. He was afraid of women. It was a question of needs.

"I used to collect stamps," he said. "I had a beautiful collection. Theresa burned it. She burned it on the day the Bolsheviks entered Germany."

Toni smiled helplessly. His eyes were hard and grey and vacant. She recognised the mood, and she was afraid.

"Is it true about you and the artist?"

"Who told you?"

"My sister."

I wonder if she reads my diary, he thought.

His eyes never left her. And in spite of herself she was excited and tingling.

"I love him," she said quickly.

"He is only a boy."

Toni wanted to conceal their bed from him. She was suddenly ashamed of her body. She would have liked, that moment, to cover herself to her fingertips. He must not see anything.

"He is no good. He drinks."

Last night, for the first time, André had made love to her with the lights on. He had studied her body lovingly and all night long he had held her in his arms. "I love you," he had said. "You are beautiful." I remember the taste of his sweat.

"You don't understand, Roger."

I hate her, he thought. He held the sheets tightly in his fists. He couldn't think of anything to say so he said: "He is a friend of the Jew."

"So am I."

Roger laughed. His laugh was short, and without humour. "Should I kill the Jews?" he asked.

Toni flushed. "He is not afraid of you."

"You are wrong. They are always afraid. Even now, when they are in power, they are afraid."

"Please go. I don't feel well," Toni said.

Roger spoke in spurts. He parted with his words grudgingly, as if they were prickly objects stuck in his throat.

"You do not understand . . . how . . . how rotten they are," he said. "Our landlord, a Polish Jew, evicted my parents from their home because . . . because they couldn't pay the rent. My father died under the knife of a Jew. It was a simple operation. He was murdered. *They plan to rule the world . . .*"

Theresa had told him about the landlord, but he was certain about the doctor. His name was Bergman.

"Oh, what do I care about the Jews!" Toni said.

"Do you live with him?"

Toni did not reply.

"He is not even a communist. I could respect him if he at least had the courage for that. But, no. He is nothing. A coward."

Toni laughed shrilly. "It is you who are afraid," she said.

"Afraid? Afraid of what?"

"Oh, I don't know!"

"Well, I'll tell you. It's their talk. Talk, talk, talk. They make a man dizzy with their talk!"

Toni turned away from him. She found a cigarette on the dresser and lit it. Now he is in his room, she thought. He is painting or looking out of the window and thinking with his forehead all creased up. *I am with him, I'm not here at all.*

"Does he give you money?"

"Why does everyone think they can be filthy with me?"

Kraus moved towards her almost sadly. He took her in his arms and she turned her face away. She felt his hand on her breast. It was a hard hand, not understanding and kind like the hand of André.

"You will never be any better than a whore with him," he said.

She struggled out of his arms. But when she saw the expression on his face she was sorry.

"I love another man."

"I love you," he said with difficulty.

Unwillingly, Toni thought: his love is realer than André's. She felt panicky. André, more than anything else, feels sorry for all of us without understanding. But Kraus looks up to me, he needs me.

"I am so tired. Tired of politics, tired of killing. You don't understand what she does to me. Oh, I hate her," he said passionately, "I could kill her."

"Roger, I'm sorry. I . . ."

Roger was pale and his face was rigid. She wished she could love him. It would be better than André.

"They all hate me for what I have done. Chaim, the men in the bars. It's her fault, she always told me what to do. I would like to be their comrade. I . . . Do you like skiing?"

His eyes were bright and unseeing. She was no longer frightened and suddenly she pulled his head to her breast. "I have never been skiing," she said.

"I am good with my hands. We could go to Germany and she would never find us. I could be a carpenter." He stopped short. "They would put me in jail, they say I killed . . ."

"Roger, you are a man. Why don't you leave her?"

Kraus laughed pathetically. "She is so strong. I hate her, but I can't leave her. Who else would talk to me? Who . . . You don't know what it is to be lonely. What if the things I did were wrong, what if the dead really weren't bad?" He held her urgently and his grip was as strong as steel. "We could go to South America, to Argentina. I have friends there."

"Roger, you don't understand. I love André. You can only be my friend."

He pushed her away and laughed hoarsely. "I do not want to be your friend!"

"There are other women. You are not a bad man, you will find . . ."

"I'm going away. I'm going, I'm going!"

"Roger!"

His face was white with anger.

"You women are strong! But I will show you and Theresa and your boy of a lover. I will show you all!"

"Roger, don't be a child."

He tried to grab her again. This time viciously, for he was a man injured. But she moved away.

"He is no good. He will be unfaithful to you."

"If he is unfaithful to me I will see what to do then. But that is my problem."

"I am a champion athlete. I have won many medals. Don't you understand, I love you!"

"Oh, Roger, please, I must get dressed now."

Kraus smiled, lasciviously, and like a boy. "I will sit here while you get dressed. I will sit here and watch."

She began to sob. "Please . . ."

"Just now you were more friendly."

"Yes, but you abuse my friendship."

Roger stood up. "You are too cheap for me anyway."

He slammed the door after him.

II

"Why has he got rat traps on the floor?"

"He was ill for a month when he came here. He hadn't been eating properly or something like that. He imagines things. Guillermo told me all about him one night. He comes from a very wealthy family."

"You would think he could afford a better room than this?"

Manuel was sprawled out on the bed and sipping cognac. García had pushed the canvas tablecloth to one side and cleared a seat for himself on the trunk. He was also drinking.

"They enjoy pretending that they are poor," Manuel said. "It broadens their education. It is romantic."

"You shouldn't talk that way. He is a good friend of Guillermo's. He has done him many favours. Perhaps he is really poor?"

"Favours? I have had enough of their charity. It stinks!"

"Still, he is a friend . . ."

"Guillermo is a romantic. Having a foreign artist for a friend appeals to the bourgeois in him."

"But . . ."

"You are a boy. You understand nothing. I know the type. They do you favours. They sympathise. The workers suffer so much. My, my. But as soon as there is a crisis, poof! – they disappear."

André opened the door and stared blankly at the two strangers. He didn't know what to think. He smiled weakly.

García jumped up. "We are friends of Guillermo's," he said shyly.

"Well then." André said, grinning broadly now, "I'm glad to have you here. Where's Guillermo? I'm sorry that I'm late. I went for a walk. I wasn't expecting him until later in the afternoon."

"He gave us this address. He said he would be here later. I hope you don't mind," García said.

"Why should he mind?" Manuel, still lolling on the bed, said dryly.

"Yes, of course," André said. "Please sit down."

"García. My name is García. This is Manuel."

"My name is Bennett."

"We know your name. We know all about you. You paint."

André picked up the bottle of cognac from the floor and poured himself a drink. He was anxious to make a good impression. "Would you like me to refill your glasses?" he said.

García smiled shyly. He was stocky and dark and probably still in his teens. He was dressed shabbily, but his clothes were obviously well taken care of. He spoke Castilian with the clipped accent of a *Mallorquín*. "If you like," he said.

André filled the glasses.

"Do you like Spain?" García asked.

Manuel laughed. He was a bony man with a hard face and mean eyes. His hair was grey. A long curving scar, probably from a knife wound, ran down his left cheek. André stared at him. Manuel smiled cynically. "It is very ugly, isn't it?"

"I'm sorry. I didn't realise that I was . . ."

"Have you ever been in prison? In one of Franco's prisons?"

"Do you like Spain?" García asked again – quickly.

"Does he like Spain? Fool! It is cheap. If you are a foreigner, Spain is cheap. The beggars are ugly, I admit, but one gets used to that."

"Do you think that Guillermo will be here soon?"

"Would you like us to leave? Do we embarrass you?"

"I didn't say that at all."

Manuel got off the bed and walked over to the easel. He poked André's unfinished canvas with his finger. There were no nails on his fingers, just black sores. "Isn't there anything more important to paint than naked women?"

"I think the woman is very beautiful," García said timidly.

"What do you know about such things!"

"Let him alone!" André said. "I'm sure he knows just as much about it as you do!"

Manuel smiled contemptuously. "That's right. What do we know about art? We aren't gentlemen. We haven't had an education."

"Stop twisting my words."

"Why do you come to Spain at all? Does it amuse you? Do you think our women make good whores? Do you think it is droll to be a young idler while better men than you die in prison?"

"Shuttup!"

Manuel turned to García and shrugged his shoulders ironically. "It disturbs the poor child to hear about such things." He patted André's cheek tenderly. "Poor unhappy artist," he said.

André pushed him away quickly.

The door opened.

"What are you doing here?"

Manuel did not turn around to face Guillermo. Instead he stared at André, his eyes cold with hatred. "Didn't you tell us to meet you here?"

"I asked you to meet me at Cosmi's," Guillermo said. "I said if I was needed you could find me here."

"Let's go," García said, tugging Manuel by the arm.

Manuel didn't protest. But he stopped at the door and bowed. "Thank you for your excellent cognac, Don André. I'm sorry if we soiled your rug."

He slammed the door after him.

André washed out a glass and poured Guillermo a drink. He moved about mechanically and in his eyes was the old expression of hurt and confusion. You build and build and build, he thought. Then bango! I should know better. I should. He lit another cigarette and sat down on the window sill. "How are you, Guillermo," he asked in English. "I haven't seen you in months."

"I've been in Madrid."

Guillermo had lost weight and his skin was yellow. A wrinkle like a jumping wire ran from his left eye down to the corner of his melancholy mouth.

"Will you be here long?"

"No. I'm going to Barcelona tomorrow. But only for a few days. Then I expect I shall be in Valencia for several months."

André said nothing. Everybody gets their part to play, he thought. We get a card with our number on it.

"He just got out last week," Guillermo said. "The last time he was saved only because the officer in charge of the firing squad decided to break up for lunch. They had been shooting for four hours without stop. He is a hero, André. He . . . well, he expected things to be different when he got out."

"Guillermo, you look like you've got jaundice. Must you go to Barcelona?"

"There is going to be a strike in Barcelona."

"But you have no arms! You have no money! The city is packed with civil guards. It's suicide, Guillermo!"

"It will be the first time we have done anything concrete since the war. Do you realise what that means?"

"Yeah. More heroes," André grinned insipidly. He felt ashamed. "Will many be killed?"

"No. Nothing like that."

Guillermo took out his tobacco pouch and rolled himself a cigarette. His hands were rough, callused, but remarkably sensitive. André remembered how he had once seen him rush across the street and save a dog from being run over at the risk of his own life. (I would never do that, he thought suddenly. I would simply turn away, cringing with fear.) And looking into his face André realised for the first time how very stern it really was. Even the eyes – tender, brilliant, angry – still stern. What goes into the making of a revolutionary?

"You can stay here tonight. I'll be staying with Toni. Don't go down to Pepe. María is pregnant. You know how excited Pepe gets when he sees you. I don't think it would be a good idea."

"All right." Guillermo got up and examined the picture on the easel. "It is a very beautiful picture, André. You seem to know so many lovely things about colour. You are a fine artist."

André refilled his glass.

"Did you ever read *The Edge*?" he asked.

"The Edge. . . ."

"Yes. It's a long poem about the defence of Madrid. Oh young comrades, and all that. It's pretty good, you know. By a man named Raymond, an American."

"Yes, I remember now."

"Isn't he a Catholic now?"

"I don't know. But I could ask him. I met him yesterday afternoon at Ruzafa's."

"They got bored with the cocktail parties in New York so they came over for the party in Spain. The ones who wrote the most moving things about Madrid never got any closer to the lines than the writer's conferences." Guillermo laughed helplessly and wrinkles showed in his forehead. I am tired, he thought. André wants me to say such things that will allow him to repudiate or label me. (If I was like Manuel it would be easier for him.) Then, completely isolated, he will be able to die his selfish death. "They switch their political favours like a woman changing petticoats. Many of them were queers, and they don't understand war or revolution. They were never truly communists or anything – just shadows. Fireflies! They come just near enough to warm their bellies, then they fly away to their pink suburban bedrooms. Life is so dirty for the aesthete!"

"What about the Lincoln Brigade?"

"All right. There was the Brigade. But your friend Raymond is much better off in the Church. There are nicer costumes, and a lot more secrets."

"You hate the Americans, I know. But the American bourgeois is no worse than any other. They have had more advantages, that's all."

If I hate them, Guillermo thought, it is for their own sake.

"I remember when you were ill," he said. "When all you knew was despair and all you did was drink. Do you know why, André? Not because of the girl and her father. That is only incidental. It is because you are without hope or reason or direction. You are *sin centimo*. If you are a humanist there is only one place for you. You must join us."

"No, dammit! Too few of our reformers have no other cause for their anger besides a basic contempt for humanity. Too . . ."

"Who do you paint for?"

"I don't think that we can be expected to kill and paint as well. I . . ." André stopped. "Perhaps you think I'm being pompous?"

"Are you a pacifist?"

André walked over to the window. I guess my crime is that I haven't chosen, he thought. I wonder what my punishment will be? And who will be my judge? Below, the unlovely buildings clung together wretchedly. A *falla* satirising bullfighters was being repaired on the street corner. The gaudy cardboard fantasy stood out in colourful contrast to the greying streets. Chaim had told him: "In America they believe in the buildings. The buildings are the lies of weak ignorant men."

"No, I am not a pacifist," André said. "I *must* act. There is a need to live – or die, if you like – nobly and with purpose. But I don't know what to do?"

"Who do you paint for?"

"I paint for the understanding."

Guillermo shrugged his shoulders. It was an old man's gesture. Not bitter and not hopeful. "We could give you the opportunity to reach an audience so far untouched. You wouldn't have to paint for the fatuous, corrupt bourgeois."

"Look, I don't paint for audiences. I don't make a hobby out of humanity and I don't collect workers. But Pepe likes my stuff. So do many of his friends. But for the most part their appreciation is a kind of snobbery, and if they were bourgeois they would have about as much use for art as their fellows. It's just as true that their tremendous concern with social justice is directly related to their own poverty and as much expected of them as is the puerility and such that we get from the bourgeois. Christ, there's nothing unusual about being a bourgeois or a worker. It is the man who is unusual – the man who rises above the restrictions of his own class to assert himself as an individual and humanitarian. It's pretty damn elementary to be aware of social injustice and poetic truth and beauty but to be capable of empathy, to understand the failings of a man – any man – even as you condemn him, well … Look, every human being is to be approached with a sense of wonder. The rest is crap, or incidental."

"Hitler was a great individualist. He said there was no substitute for personality."

"Christ! that's not fair."

"Individuality! When a man has enough bread then he can worry about being an individual. You talk like an anarchist!"

"Dammit, Guillermo! Will you get it through your head that I am nothing. Not an anarchist. Not a communist. Not a fascist. Nothing."

"I'm afraid that's nineteenth century, André. You will be killed. It is the will of society and unavoidable. Even if it is only a symbolic death."

"There are worse things to die for than beauty."

"There are better things. Humanity."

"Aren't they the same?"

"We think so."

"So do I. But we see things differently."

"People are hungry. There can be no misunderstanding about that."

André swallowed his cognac, and grunted. He paced up and down the room smoking. He thought: Panic is shaped like a tree and all the branches reach for you. Panic is the chill on the lips of the young. Panic is shot from guns. (It doesn't happen to the Best People. Nothing happens to the Best People. Why? Because they change their ideas. They salt away money for rainy days. They don't learn new tricks and they subscribe to the Thought of the Week. For the Best People life is just a B movie.)

"Are you going to marry Toni?"

"Why do you ask?"

"Aren't you in love with her?"

"Sometimes I don't know." André lit another cigarette off his butt and laughed nervously. "Love? . . . today we come together out of mutual desperation."

"I have to go now, André. The others will be waiting for me at Cosmi's."

"Are you angry?"

"No. Of course not."

"Will you have supper with me?"

"I can't, André. I'm sorry. But when I get back I hope that we will see each other often."

No, André thought. We won't see each other often. He feels only pity for me – I am the End and he is the Beginning. Chaim? Chaim comes after, when he will be needed. *God knows he will be needed!* For Guillermo is only capable of destruction.

"Take care of yourself, Guillermo. Don't be a hero."

Guillermo got up. He took a thick notebook out of his breast pocket. "I wrote some poems. Would you like to read them?"

"Yeah, sure."

"I'll leave them with you."

"Great, I'll do some drawings for them."

"They are communist poems. They will be printed in our paper."

"When you get back let's do a book together. I haven't done any engravings for a long time. We could print it ourselves. I think it would be fun."

"We shall talk about it again." Guillermo smiled awkwardly. "Well. So long. Thanks for the drinks."

André grinned self-consciously. "Aren't you going to apologise for dirtying my rug?"

"Don't joke about it. Please."

"Why not? Everything is a joke. It has to be."

III

Guitarist whining, whining:

> *Ay! puerto moro de Tanger;*
> *Ay! ya no te veo más;*
> *Ay! ay, ay, ay,*
> *Ay! que no te puedo olvidar.*

Eyes of burning coal. Sweat running down leather cheeks. Fingers beating on a guitar. Beating, beating, beating. Head in a coma, head in a spell. Fluid body swaying. Twangy guitar sending up a burst of metal song:

> *Fuego! Fuego! Fuego!*

The Andalusian dancer, a beautiful homosexual from Seville, stamps his small feet furiously down on the floor. Waving his arms through the air he entices his sweating partner into a deeper ecstasy; clacking her castanets with a brilliant perfection the dark girl abandons herself completely, winding and unwinding her body in quickening raptures. . . .

A song of great pain freely flowing.

"*Olé!*"

The excited rhythmic clapping of men and women enchanted by the naked dance of their souls performing.

The crowd shouts: "*Fuego! Fuego! Fuego!*"

Mad guitar raving! Ten joy-crazy soulfingers swooping down on the strings bonily.

"*Venga hombre!*"

"*Venga! Venga!*"

Backwards bending, down, down, bends the dark girl. Castanets clacking clear and hard. The sweat-soaking boy, hands clapping loud overhead, stamps around her triumphantly. Up she dances, body panting, hair flowing.

"*Fuego! Fuego! Fuego!*"

Guitar exhausted, fingers dying on strings, dancers slowing to a stop, clacking, feet now beating softly . . .

The music stops.

All applaud. "*Olé! Olé!*"

"Christ! They really get their water hot, huh? I never saw people get so excited over a dance," Barney said.

"They're Spanish! Didn't you know? Didn't I tell you they're Spanish?"

Derek tittered. I hate you, Barney, he thought. You live in an official world of official lives and official deaths and official loves. I am unofficial and dark so I hate you. Derek reconsidered his thoughts and again he tittered. In our awfully arty villa in Tourettes, Jon is strutting up and down and thinking of throwing himself into the ravine. He won't do it because he is a coward. With me it is different, I wasn't always a coward. *I hate him too*, he thought. He turned to Jessie. "It's too bad Mama isn't with us," he said. "Wouldn't she simply adore that small-assed dancer?"

Jessie scowled. "Stop it, you fool. You're drunk!"

"That was very typical. Now we should dance ourselves," Juanito said. "Would you like me to arrange for two other girls to join us?"

"Now that would be damn nice!" Barney said.

Juanito arranged his tie, smoothed back his sleek black hair, and disappeared through the velvet backdrop of the booth.

"He's really a good guy! Sometimes you can tell about people on the first meeting."

Jessie arranged her tufty auburn hair. "He has wonderful teeth," she said.

Derek smirked.

They had met Juanito in the hotel. Apparently he was a visiting textile salesman from Madrid and knew Valencia intimately. After supper they had had a few cognacs together in the bar and Juanito had suggested they visit a typical Valencian cabaret. He had carried himself with such aplomb, made his suggestions so decorously, that none of them had the will to resist him. Then he had particularly endeared himself to Barney by listening attentively to his political dissertations on Spain, emphatically agreeing with him that if nothing else, Franco had ingeniously imposed order on a nation of anarchists.

Ushering in two attractive girls before him, Juanito re-entered the booth. The girls appeared so much alike – flowing black hair, portentous black eyes under heavy lids, full lips and good figures – that they might easily have been sisters. They smiled shyly, professionally unprofessional.

"This is Carmen." Juanito grinned at the girl in the green dress. "And this is María."

He said something to them in Spanish and they sat down. Barney offered them each a glass of champagne which they gratefully accepted.

"Shall we dance?" Juanito asked, still grinning.

"Nothing like the present."

But Barney was not of the present. This, at long last, was one of his European experiences. He was already thinking of the evening in terms of how he would embellish on it over cocktails for the benefit of the boys at the lodge several months hence.

"Will you allow me the pleasure of dancing with the beautiful *señora*?" Juanito asked.

"Certainly."

"Which whore is mine?" Derek asked.

"Sometimes you make me sick!"

Because of the heat the men abandoned their jackets before they left the booth.

Juanito, even with his satisfactory talents, fell into difficulties wheeling his tipsy partner about the floor.

From the bar André watched the swarming couples jerk their bodies in sympathy with the samba. Although he was loathe to admit it, he was grateful for this bit of America, as it was, superimposed on the catastrophe of Spain. His breakdown, even as his first childhood tantrum . . .

– The headaches are purely imaginary. I'm afraid, Mrs. Bennett, the child is abnormally high-strung.

– Oh, doctor, I'm sure it is his artistic background coming out.

. . . had seemed like the last explosion, the merciful explosion after which self-destruction would be complete, no more headaches after.

Later, he knew, Juanito would summarise this evening's exploits for him with a long eloquent harangue apropos of what magnificent idiots were all Americans. Of course, excluding André, who was, after all, a great, great artist. Hadn't Chaim told them? Didn't he have the letter from the great Gibbins in his pocket to prove it?

". . . and the canvas discovered by Mr. Fitzpatrick in the Student's Union, *The Agony*, shows a great and original talent. . . . more than promising. . . .

'If you will ship us posthaste whatever pictures you have done in Paris, and fill out the enclosed contract authorising Kendell Galleries to act as your agent in New York, I can more than assure you . . ."

The Canadian artists! Mediocrity draped in the maple leaf! Sonnets by the ageing virgin grand-daughters of Tory tradesmen evoking the memories of rather un-Presbyterian passions, slick paintings by sophisticates with a shrewd eye turned towards New York. Kultchir, ladies! Step right up and get yur goddam Kultchir while it's real hot! Kultchir as celebrated by imperial favour annually consisting of fifty gold guineas for the horse that wins the King's Plate and an honorary award for either virgin poetess or pipe-smoking historian-novelist.

So damn their contracts! Paint for whom?

Chaim refilled the glasses.

"You should have seen me, André. It was really so goddam funny. Me, a pale greenhorn with questioning *Yiddish* eyes landed in New York. America, America! I ran away from home and joined a *Yiddish* comedy troupe as a singer of hymns. I left them in St. Louis. I must have been all of sixteen then. Sidecurls, and Old World illusions, clipped and fallen on the blazing asphalt of progress, I wandered like a tramp over the bullshit of the American wilderness. Salesman, dishwasher, cabbie, jobber. When the depression came I was properly screwed. All the money I had with me went towards buying a plot of earth for my mother and a husband for my sister."

"But I thought you were in Paris during the depression?"

Chaim shoved a cigar into André's breast pocket. "Tell me, *boychick*," he said, fingering André's lapel contemptuously, "you call that a suit?"

"You told me that story."

André had shaved. His seedy brown hair was combed flatly back on his head, making him look something of the young fool and something of the well-brought-up young idler. It was this physical proof of his privileged past that failing to absorb and define he hoped to uproot by method-ical abuse of his person, by unbuttoned collars and unshined shoes, by hair uncombed and face unshaven. Not knowing that he could not sever himself from his past but instead could absorb it intelligently.

"No. I didn't leave America until after the death of Rebecca," Chaim said. "Didn't I ever tell you about my Rebecca? My God, it's been more than twenty years now! We worked in the same sweatshop and I was very much in love with her. I won't bother you with all kinds of details and complications, but at the time I was a very earnest revolutionary. Then one night a comrade who had been thrown out of work said to me: 'Sometimes, Chaim, I wish I had a machine-gun. Then I would go out and shoot every goddam capitalist who thought that the only way to solve a problem was through war.'"

"That has nothing to do with the party."

"No. But it proved that I wasn't a revolutionary."

The band stopped playing. Slowly the sweaty couples cleared the floor, slinking back to their tables unwillingly.

"I loved her very much, André. When she died I returned to the Warsaw ghetto. I read all night and during the day I repaired shoes. I must be boring the hell out of you. Who wants to listen to an old man's memories?

"You," he waggled a finger at him, "can, if you choose, sit up all night and paint, but I am too old. The organism doesn't respond. When I was your age, death was just a funny story, but now I'm fat and vulnerable and the joke has become a threat."

"Chaim, they're going to get you in bits. Five more years and poof! out with the prostate gland."

Chaim belched loudly. "If you were a Jew I'd tell you where to get off that remark. As it is I have respect for the *Goyim*."

"Talking about the *Goyim*," André said absently, "do you know anything about the German? The one who's always in the club."

"Kraus? His sister is the brains of the family. He's a pretty dumb bastard himself. Sometimes I give him work smuggling cigarettes from Palma. I like to have him run messages for me. It makes me feel like a Cossack. Why do you ask?"

"He seems to be everywhere I go. Maybe I'm afraid of him?"

Chaim drained his glass, rolling the wine on his tongue. "Don't get mixed up with him. Keep out of his way."

Chaim refilled the glasses and André yawned.

The band idled back on stage and began to fiddle with their instruments. The lachrymose pianist, his pin-point eyes way out of focus, giggled foolishly. The bandleader, a gaunt morose-looking man, yanked the cigarette out of his mouth. The others laughed.

"I wish I could paint like you. I mean that."

"It's always wrong to kill, isn't it?" André asked suddenly.

Chaim lit a cigar. "Why did the priests teach that the sun goes around the earth?"

"That's no answer."

"You were very ill. You had a bad breakdown, so don't . . ."

"Please, Chaim. I'm okay now."

"Well don't talk like a *yold* then."

André swung around on the bar stool to see if he could find Toni.

Chaim plucked the cigar from his lips. "You want another cognac?"

"Okay. But just one."

A cognac was ordered from Luís.

"The good word, according to our friend Juanito, is that God is dead," André said. "He also says that the money-changers have inherited the earth."

Chaim scratched his balding head and chuckled. "Juanito is a *shmock*. His forte is egoism, women. As a wit he is only a Spaniard."

"He's not such a bad guy."

Chaim waved his arms in the air indicating dismissal. "His father was a great surgeon and a good man," Chaim said. "His mother came from the aristocracy, but the hard way if you know what I mean. About eight times removed. I guess her mother changed the dressings on Alfonso's piles. Something like that. Juanito is the butt-end."

André slapped his thighs and laughed.

"An ignorant man," Chaim began earnestly, "cherishes another man's sin because . . ."

"Don't be so solemn. This is fiesta! Spain! Music! Do you want them to cancel your B'nai Brith card?"

"Do you want to hear a story about Rabbi Akiba?"

"You're always telling me stories about Rabbi Akiba or Hillel."

"But we're getting places, don't you see? Without Hillel there couldn't have been Christ. Without Christ who knows what might have been? Chaos? But that's what we've got now, isn't it? For hundreds of years men have murdered in the name of Christ. It's a contradiction, isn't it? Killing *for* God? Isn't anything you can kill for bad?"

"Okay," André said impatiently, "nothing is good."

"Man is good. He made God. Christ was good too. It's the Christians that stink! But Christ was proud and that's why he was crucified. That's why you're so melancholy sometimes, because you're proud. That's why Moses never got to the Promised Land, because he was proud.

"Judas was good too. You know what really happened? Christ was getting prouder and prouder. He thought he was so good people had to wash his feet when he sat down. Imagine allowing another man to wash your feet! Judas was his best friend. Jesus kept saying over and over again to Judas I'm the Son of God and very holy, God will never let me die. And Judas said like hell you are! Everybody is the Son of God and we all die and return to Him. No, Jesus said, I'm special. Nobody is special before God, Judas said. Not even you! So they made a bet. Jesus said you go tell the Romans where I am and they'll come to crucify me but in the last moment God won't let me die because I'm His Son. And Judas wept. We said, you'll die, Jesus. You'll die. But Jesus was proud and he insisted. So Judas went. And the Romans came and got Jesus. When Pilate said to the people should I let him go? They said, no! no! And in a way they were right because Jesus was always making them feel guilty and ashamed because they were human instead of godly. So poor Jesus was crucified and he died. And Judas knew that no Son of God was that important. The rest of the story is all fantasy."

"Oh, that's just crap, Chaim. You don't really believe it."

"Believe it? But the story doesn't matter. It is the idea of the story that is true and important."

André thought he saw Toni dancing with the German and he was angry.

"Tell me, André. Sometimes I wonder what's wrong with you kids. You seem to build everything around a circle, and the circle is empty. What do you believe in?"

André laughed shyly. "I guess more than anything else we believe in not believing."

"But that doesn't mean anything."

André frowned. "I feel uneasy," he said.

"Why?"

"I don't know. Toni looks at me sometimes as if she expects me to pop off or be shot any moment. She makes me nervous."

"Don't worry. She probably thinks she's a gypsy. They all do."

Softly she kissed him on the lips.

He was pleasantly surprised. They had dallied with each other for a bit without him meeting with the coy rebukes that he was so accustomed to. (Secretly he wished André was in the booth so that he might see for himself what a maestro was his friend Juanito.) In a hoarse voice he whispered the classical Spanish endearments which poor Jessie failed to comprehend. She was embarrassed by the incongruity of his passion.

"Perhaps we should dance?"

"Your lips are poetry and your eyes full of moons of love." He embraced her tightly. Long, lingering kiss.

"Spanish men are such great lovers. All the foreign ladies ..."

"I'd better go and fix my face before the others get back."

"Poor, lost Juanito." He lowered his eyes. "His soul burns with such a love, his heart ..."

She kissed him lightly on the forehead, rather like one reprimands a somewhat naughty child, and disappeared through the curtain.

Juanito sulked. Resentfully he watched Barney shove María about the floor. Derek held on to Carmen as if she disgusted him, and he was not even following the music. It is late, Juanito thought. And we haven't even consumed much champagne with those *crudos* dancing all the time! Barney's sport jacket fell to the floor and Juanito bent down to pick it up. The wallet fell out.

When had Barney possessed her as a lover? They had made a deal, and that was it. Still, Barney had money, so why force him into a divorce? She gave her hair one last delicate pat and gazed at her reflection in the mirror. Yes, at thirty-five she still had a fine figure, much more to offer a man than any nasty child of nineteen. She had been wise to insist on only two children.

Perhaps because she detected the first sagging lines of age on her neck she turned sharply away from the mirror.

When she stepped out of the powder room she noticed André idling at the bar. He seemed so intent on something. The admonished child – told No by his parents but not Why. A deep tenderness for him swelled within her. Encouraged by this rare honesty she walked towards him slowly.

"Why didn't you keep your appointment, André?"

"I don't like your brother," he said.

"He's just a spoilt child. No good perhaps, but harmless all the same."

She wanted badly to say I want to be kind, I want to be nice – but she didn't know how to express it.

Jessie wandered through life not experiencing things but accumulating memories. One day she would be old and men would find her body ugly. In preparation for this she was collecting episodes, a book of satisfactions over which she could ruminate when she was no longer a desirable woman. So all happenings were snatched at greedily, double-taken, and not honestly enjoyed. She did not guess that instead of remembering her "memories" she might only be able to recall the unfilled intervals between, the duds, the awful blanks.

"You don't get along with your family, do you?" she asked.

"No."

"Are they really wealthy?"

"Very."

"So was my father. He was a very great man. A banker. He was one of those people who was just too good to live. He died quite suddenly in the early days of the New Deal. We could have faced the bank auditors together if not for my mother. She made life unbearable for him. And then she was always so fussy about Derek." She smiled kindly. "I was in Canada once."

"Did you see any beavers?"

The bar stool he sat on was high. She leaned up against his knees.

"Your buttons are undone."

"Button them for me."

He did up the buttons slowly. The feel of her breasts tingled on the backs of his fingers.

"Why don't you come to New York? Take Barney's offer of a job."

"For one thing I haven't got enough money for a train ticket to Paris." Guillermo is right, he thought. I am without hope or reason or direction.

"If I ask him he'll buy you a boat ticket."

Her voice was still soft, but unsubtle also. An implement studied in the seduction of bored lawyers and doctors with frigid career wives.

Suddenly André burst out laughing. "Hey, you must really clean up in the U.S., eh?"

She giggled. "Will you come?" she asked.

André considered her offer. Back to America – the done version of a bum world already gone bad. Slogan thoughts and tabloid ideas, a bedside Freud and a billboard neurosis. He had the letter from Norman in his pocket: "WHO AM I AND WHY AM I HERE? Ask yourself this daily *for you are running away*." And of course, the suburban sophisticates – Saturday night is beer and ideas, talk cozy with intellectual commonplaces. *We are the enlightened!* We are SUFFERING for the *rotters*, the *stinkers*, the people who lead such boring godawful lives not like us at all (Warren, darling, please play those Eliot records again, I'm worried about the meaning). O God, O Christ! *America is a furnace and the temperature is 180 F and still going up. Men in rimless glasses and women in slacks are stoking and stoking and if you don't wear a white-Protestant-imgoingplaces-TV-B.A.-Luce-rugged nonentity uniform, then in the fire with you – Rogue!* . . . Another rented room, long walks at night on the cold neon-lit desert, pretty girls just pretty in their summer print dresses. . . .

"I'm evading the draft."

"Are you a Red?"

She said it unemotionally. Not alluding to its political implications, but as if being a Red could be embarrassing, like someone in the family having an illegitimate child.

André hesitated. "I'm not even a pacifist. I just don't want to die foolishly."

"Are you a coward?"

"Something like that."

"I don't understand politics. Join us for a glass of champagne?"

"Okay."

She squeezed his hand.

Juanito frowned when André entered the booth. He appeared nervous. The two Spanish girls were nowhere around.

Barney grinned merrily. "Hiya! What gives?" he asked.

André hoped that Barney wasn't drunk. He was sorry now that he had accepted Jessie's invitation. He looked out across the dance floor but he couldn't see Toni. He wondered if she was watching him.

Juanito poured André a glass of champagne. "André and myself are great friends. We met in Madrid," he said.

Juanito resented André's intrusion. He felt that André finding him here like this – lying, entertaining *crudos* – might interpret the situation so as to establish his own superiority over Juanito.

In his corner Derek moped with bellicose deliberation. He had none of the pure lines that imposed a wicked grace on his sister's face. Only the family malice. He resembled a roguish caricature of Jessie. "Ah!" he said, smiling drunkenly, "my fan club has arrived – the man who read *The Edge*. Tell me, old boy, did you have an unhappy childhood? Do you think I'm a bit of a cliché by now? Well don't make snap judgements, you know absolutely nothing about it. *Homme, je suis.* . . . You too, Canada, may turn out to be *only* intelligent, *just* bright. Meanwhile, I shall be generous, I grant you licence to hate me. Why not?"

André flushed. "I've got an idea, Derek. Why don't you try feeling sorry for yourself. Drink, go to pot! That's what always happens in the movies."

Derek laughed bitterly. He recalled, dimly at first, the last of the parties on the terrace of Jimmy's Bar in Haut de Cagnes. Most of the fags had worn falsies under their costumes and Lila had turned up in a tuxedo. Jon had disgraced him again. Now, it came back to him vividly – the sweet music, contaminated laughter, sad adolescents doodling with deviations, night air stinking of summer and sea, the tourists up from Cannes for kicks. He felt dizzy and lonely and disgusted. "*Ça va*, Canada. . . . I withdraw. At your age everything is still possible." I will write to Jon, he thought, and advise him to jump into the ravine. He turned to Jessie. "I've had too much to drink. I feel sick."

Jessie leaned on André's arm. "We're touched," she said.

"Let's dance, Jessie," Derek said.

"André has already asked me for this dance."

"Dance with me! I want to talk to you."

"Dance with him!" Barney said.

Clumsily Derek directed Jessie out of the booth. Barney brightened up as soon as they were gone.

"Look, kid, this is the score," Barney said hastily, his eyes bulging with conspiracy. "We're going to get Jessie off to the hotel and dump her in bed. Juanito here is going to show us what really goes on in this town. He's going to line us up with some broads! You come back to the hotel with us and we'll meet Juanito here in about an hour. Okay?"

"Okay, I guess."

Juanito averted his eyes.

"I'll pay the bill," Barney said.

Juanito jumped to his feet. "No! No! Allow me to pay."

André laughed nervously.

IV

Derek remained in the café downstairs sipping coffee and composing notes for his letter to Jon. Barney had disappeared down the hall in search of a toilet.

The room in the hotel was small and obvious.

Jessie paced up and down the floor puffing furiously on a cigarette. André relaxed on the bed, also smoking.

"You think I'm drunk!"

Her hair, which she had attended to so faithfully all evening, had finally unruffled itself, falling in angry curls over her round forehead. She was beautiful now – passion compensating for lost youth, dangling curls blending with the heat of her eyes.

"You think I'm drunk?"

"You should be drunk."

Before they had persuaded Jessie to abandon the Mocambo Club they had had to allow her three quick shots of cognac. Now, her latest whim was, she would not go to bed until she had had a private conversation with André.

Stomping up and down the room she appeared to be stalking an absent beast.

And it's all been done before, André thought. The young artist and the bored Mrs. Whatsit abroad for the first time.

Only the poets in fact perpetually disagree as to who seduces whom. What perversion of curiosity brought me here when I really want to be with Toni? Okay, so she's hot stuff. But why do I always allow myself to drift into a situation, why do I always lack the guts to pull out when it's time?

"You're just a child!"

"Maybe."

"A nasty, ungrateful child."

Looking out of the window, he could see into the darkness of the plaza, just above where he knew was the doomed wooden *falla*, still leering. "You are without hope or reason or direction." Not if I act.

She turned on him angrily. "How old are you?" she asked.

"Twenty-three."

"Is that all? And how long have you been painting?"

"About ten years."

"Is your painting any good?"

"Good enough to have been suppressed twice."

She flung her cigarette to the floor and ground it to bits with her heel. A shudder ran through her body, very much as if some inner string had been pulled, and as if by pulling it she surrendered her self-control. The moment will be mine, she thought. Even if it is no good it will be mine. Mine, always.

"I don't understand modern art."

"Must you stomp up and down the room like that? You don't understand modern art. You feel proud and superior about it. What in the hell do you expect us to do? Stop painting just because you don't understand?"

You are a weakling, he thought. Take it out on her, that's right.

"Can you support yourself with your painting?"

"No."

She lit another cigarette. "I'll ask Barney to buy a few. Just tell me how much you want for them."

"Barney can't have any. He wouldn't understand them."

"Aren't you the proud one? I suppose in your childish mind you think it's quite an accomplishment not to be able to earn a living?"

She is an American woman, he thought. No dental odours, armpits shaven, no facial hairs, birthmarks removed in early childhood. No possibilities of human smells.

"You're just as bad as Derek," she said.

"If you mean that we both don't fit in, then yes."

She whirled about suddenly. A lock of hair fell over her forehead.

"Now, now, Jessie dear. Don't panic. I can assure you that the best of American society looks upon my sexual appetites with nothing but approval."

Jessie walked over to the window. "God, that *falla* makes me nervous!" she said.

"Tomorrow night they're going to burn all the *fallas*. It's the *Día de San José*."

And now André remembered how as a child he used to dodge his governess to run off by himself in the newly fallen snow. As he would trample in the freshly fallen snow he used to say to himself: André Bennett, you are the first person in the world to step in this snow since it fell from heaven and God.

"You miss your father, don't you?" he asked.

"Get off my bed!"

Grinning shyly, he stood up. He brushed her hair back from her forehead. "Your buttons are undoing again," he said.

"I undid them."

"Christ! Not now."

She folded her arms about his neck, holding the hurt of his melancholy head, grasping his hair tightly in her hands. Slowly she pulled his head down towards her own. Her mouth was urgent. Her eyes were shut. He held her in a half-hearted embrace.

And the stink of his sweat, the feeling of his damp shirt, ran through her, kindling flames. The tensions relaxed. The heaving and turmoil of her body sweetened. She lingered limply in his arms.

He let go of her.

"You're trying to get rid of me!"

But her body had been soft, resilient; her mouth warm.

"No. I'm not."

Her wet brown eyes filled with hatred. "I know where that *Yid* is taking you," she said. "Or did you think I was a Jew as well as Barney?"

André laughed. "I knew you were okay the moment I saw you," he said.

"What has he got to give a whore? He's only curious. He can't even . . ."

"With luck he'll catch himself a dose. That'll fix the *Yid* bastard."

"Look, pretend you're going. Agree with them. Then come back here to me."

"No. I'm sorry."

She clung to him again. "You have to come! I can't start and stop. I just can't! It drives me crazy. I won't be able to sleep."

"I . . . There's someone I have to . . ."

She dug her fingernails into the back of his neck. "Do I have to beg you?" she asked.

"Look, I have to . . ."

"Don't be afraid." Her voice had gone husky. "From here we can go to your place. They'll never know."

"No. I can't."

She kissed him pleadingly now.

"Do I remind you of your father?"

She pulled away from him and slapped him sharply across the face.

"Don't be filthy!"

Dizzily he held on to her – remembering he loved Toni, remembering Ida who was out of reach, remembering his mother who was hardly a bit more subtle than Jessie, remembering other women, other embraces. Nausea suddenly swept over him. Everything rising upwards to his throat.

"Hit me like I hit you," she whispered throatily.

"Later."

"Now, now!"

The door opened.

"Damn it!" she said. "Damn it!"

Barney absorbed the scene instantaneously. His big vulgar face was angry and beaten and afraid. But he just stood there, hanging on to the door, whimpering like a scared animal. Always coming down on him, his house-of-cards life.

"I didn't see you come in," André said, smiling feebly.

Barney laughed and laughed. Exultant, and sorrowful also.

"Please let go of the door. Please don't stand there like that."

Barney's knuckles were white around the door-knob. I am as bad as her, André thought. I don't want to see him cry.

"If you so much as touch him you'll never see me again!" Jessie screamed.

"Please . . ."

This would thrill them, this would make them happy, Barney thought. Go marry her. A Gentile! Nothing good will ever come of it. Only sadness. For us Jews, only sadness.

"You don't understand. I . . ."

"Get out!" Barney shoved him towards the door. "Tramp!"

Still protesting, André left. He shut the door behind him.

Barney collapsed in a chair and lit a cigarette. His hands shook badly. He was sweating. My children have *their* names, he thought. I don't drink, I'm not like them. "*So look, Berel. I'm warning you for always. Marry that girl and you don't step into this house again. Is this what for I came to America? So my sons . . .*"

"Get out, you!"

"Why? What did I do?" His voice was breaking. "Was it my fault?"

"Was it my fault?" Jessie giggled hysterically. "What a man I've got for a husband! Go, beat it! Go find yourself a whore. I haven't enough patience for your fumbling tonight. Get out!"

"I won't go. I have certain rights."

Her buttons are undone, Barney noticed.

"Beat it!"

"Where will I sleep? I'm so tired."

"Get out, dammit!"

He rushed out of the room.

V

So many stars shining down from the black sky, so many laughing shivering eyes.

Barney sat down on the kerb and waited.

VI

He sat down at the bar.

The big German with unfeeling eyes and big brutal hands was following Toni about like a lap-dog. She kept pushing away his hands from her as she spoke. "You must speak to him, André," Toni said. "He is crying like a child in the booth."

André gargled his coffee before swallowing. He noticed that Toni's lipstick was smudged. The big German was grinning. His arm was around Toni's waist. He was trying to drag her away from André.

Toni toyed with André's shirt collar. "He says he will commit suicide. And his blood will be on our hands," she said.

"Your lipstick is smudged."

Toni bit her lip. "Shall I get him?"

"No. Not yet."

The German smiled stiffly at André: as if, since they were both gentlemen, certainly André would have sufficient tact not to further insinuate his company upon himself and the young lady.

"You're Colonel Kraus. You seem to be everywhere I go," André said absently.

Kraus straightened up, stiffened, satisfying some inner compulsion. He understood the situation. Bowing coldly, he extended his hand. "I am very charmed to meet you," he said.

André laughed, but he shook hands. "Well, I'm damned if I know what to say." He grinned at Toni and then back at Kraus. "How are you?"

Toni was angry. She knew André when he was in that mood.

"I know all about you," Kraus said in English.

"You are the second person who has said that to me today." André remembered Manuel's hands, black sores instead of nails. "You don't look so tough, Colonel. Do you collect lampshades? What kind of soap do you use?"

Up until that moment Kraus had been following André simply because he was bored and had been trained to hunt men. Also, he had enjoyed or loved Toni and André was a rival. But now that he had actually spoken to André he realised that he was afraid of him, and that he would have to do something about it. He did not know why he was afraid of André. He had not been afraid of Alfred. He had met Guillermo and he was not afraid of him. Perhaps it was that Guillermo knew and understood and hated him for the crimes he had committed, but André – although he pretended belief – could not truly believe that men did such things. So when he looked at Kraus his eyes were full of shock. And Kraus was forced to remember, if only dimly, so many other shocked eyes out of the past. Actually, it was not the eyes he remembered but his own feeling of bewilderment. A feeling that only now, because of this quick contact with André, was assuming the shape of guilt. André, perhaps, was his accuser.

Kraus looked pained, as if he had heard what had been said but didn't quite know how to reply. "I want this girl," he said. "I want you to stop seeing her."

"What?" André said, more amazed than anything else.

"You are bad for her."

"Are you serious?"

"I do not joke."

André stared at him. Bullet-shaped head, iron-grey eyes under no brows to speak of, bad lips, a kind of mad intensity to the face, no neck, head slightly cocked and puzzled, barrel chest and no stomach but legs weak and spindly, fists curled in angry balls. "Go away, Kraus. *Vamos.* F—— off! *Allez!*"

Kraus drew his arm more firmly about Toni's waist. A sarcastic question mark settled on his face. He cocked his head. "I beg your pardon, young man?" he said.

André scowled. He was as angry with himself as he was with Kraus. "Aw look!" he said. "I don't want to fight you. That would be silly. Just go away. Leave Toni and myself alone."

Kraus stepped back – as if in just another second he was going to lunge at André.

"You are making fun of me."

"Oh, go away!"

Toni looked imploringly at André. She knew something was wrong, but she failed to understand their English.

"I beg your pardon?"

Nausea swept over André. Physical fear. A lump bobbed up and down in his throat.

"I beg your pardon?"

"This is crazy. Let's not fight, eh?"

"Are you a man or a mouse?"

André laughed.

"COBARDE."

The band looked up. The few straggling couples on the floor stopped dancing. Waiters stopped in their tracks as if caught by a jerky camera. Everything was quiet.

Kraus's words echoed around him. I beg your pardon I beg your pardon I beg your I beg – *cobarde.*

André pulled back his right fist and aimed for the spot just behind Kraus' head. Kraus ducked and the punch rolled off his cheek. Swiftly he smashed André in the face with his huge fist. He stepped back as André came toppling down, the stool falling on top of him, banging him on the head.

Toni shrieked. She beat Kraus wildly on the chest with her tiny fists. Kraus took out a handkerchief and wiped his face. He knocked Toni's fists away gently. The ring on his left hand was bloody. "I am not in the habit of brawling in bars . . . brawling with boys . . ." he said. "I am sorry, *señorita* Toni. But he is Evil."

André scrambled to his feet quickly. His nose was bloody and he could taste the blood in his mouth. Before Toni could grab him he charged wildly into Kraus, hitting him solidly to the stomach. Kraus swung his fist down, backwards, like a pendulum, smashing it into André's face on the upswing. André was swept backwards on the strength of the blow, stumbling over the fallen stool, falling backwards to the floor head first.

"Go! Please go!"

"I'm sorry. For a boy he is . . ."

Toni pushed him. "Haven't you done enough?"

Kraus started as if to say something. Then he turned around, walking out of the club.

André got up dizzily. He squinted, shook his head, then started for the door. Toni grabbed him. He felt her body jerk with sobs in his arms. André forced himself to grin. "I'm all right. I'm fine. All I need is a coffee," he said.

"Luís!"

Luís placed a cup of coffee and a cognac on the bar. André bent down to recover the stool. He toppled for an instant and then he regained his balance slowly. All around the club people were watching him. His head was swimming. His nose stung.

"I really beat the hell out of him, didn't I?" he said.

Toni laughed. Her eyes were wet. "Your nose is bleeding. Let's go, darling," she said.

André had difficulty keeping her in focus.

"Darling! Let's go."

"If Juanito wants to see me . . ."

He pressed a handkerchief to his nose. Everything felt mushy.

"I'll get him."

André swallowed his cognac swiftly. Luís handed him a cigarette and lit it for him.

André turned around but Toni was already gone.

"Do you want another cognac?" Luís asked.

"No."

André explored his mouth with his tongue. His teeth seemed all there but his tongue was raw.

"You shouldn't have done it."

"I know."

"You were wrong, André."

"I had to hit him."

"Why?"

"All I know is I had to hit him. Toni doesn't even come into it. Not the way you think anyway. I would always have to hit him."

André knocked the coffee over with his arm.

"Does your face hurt?" Luís asked pouring out another cup of coffee.

"Yes."

"Chaim will be angry."

"The hell with Chaim." He pulled the handkerchief away from his nose. "Is your . . . is my face swollen?"

"Yes."

"Is it cut?"

"No."

André laughed happily. "Jesus, I feel good!" he said.

"He fought with Franco, the son of a bitch."

"Are your glad I hit him?"

"You were wrong."

"Are you glad?"

"His sister was here yesterday. She came to see Chaim. I served her a drink. She wants me to come up to her house and repair some furniture. But don't worry, that's all. She thinks because I'm poor I'm not proud or I don't understand."

Juanito sat down at the bar. His eyes were swollen. His hair was carefully tangled up.

"What happened? Toni is crying," he said.

"I just beat up Colonel Kraus."

"I'll kill him for you!"

"Yeah, I know. Would you like some coffee?"

"Yes."

"Luís!"

"Was he able to walk out?"

"Look, Juanito, fix your hair. Comb it. I promise I'll feel sorry for you whatever it is."

Quickly Juanito brushed back his hair. "Did you hurt him badly?" he asked.

"Three waiters had to carry him out. Concussion. Five ribs smashed. I doubt if he'll pull through."

"No!"

"It was André's fault!"

Juanito handed André a cigarette and smiled intimately. "Luís is just a bartender," he said. "What could you expect him to know about such things?"

André frowned. He noticed Luís move away from them. "Well, Juanito," he said, "what happened?"

Juanito dropped a crisp one hundred dollar bill on the bar. There were a few new creases in it.

André laughed incredulously. "No! You didn't!" he said.

"Please, you must give it back to them. They'll soon be here to meet me. I mustn't be here when they come." He pushed the bill towards André. "Hurry! Take it!"

"They aren't coming."

André picked up the bill and thought of how he might get back to London with it. Go to Tangier or take Toni to Paris. Maybe even stake himself until he got a job or an exhibition together. Suddenly he thrust the note back at Juanito. "You took it, now keep it," he said.

Juanito cringed, slinking away from the bill as if it had occult powers all its own. "I believed we were friends, men of the world, we . . ."

"Dammit, Juanito. Come off it!"

"I am a gentleman. My father was a great doctor."

Juanito has made his choice and I have made mine, André thought. He is a dishonest thief and I am an officious clown – we are, both of us, expendables; waste-products.

"Listen, Juanito. Your father is dead. You are no longer a gentleman but a pimp. And a thief as well."

"Temporarily in the employ of a cabaret, perhaps. But a pimp, a thief?" He hissed the words as if terrified by their sounds. "I was an honours student at the university."

André felt that the onus of the crime had fallen on him. He shoved the bill into his pocket. "Okay. I'll give it back to him tomorrow." It will be funny too, he thought. Hey, Barney, old boy, here boy, nice boy, here jump! a hundred bucks.

Juanito embraced André. "My friends, what a gentleman! *Gracias, gracias.*"

André laughed shyly. "I'm sorry for all the rotten things I said."

"I'll go and get Toni," Juanito said.

"Wait."

But Juanito was gone.

André began to probe his scalp for bumps.

It was late. Only a few people were strewn about the club. Sipping on the dregs of their cognac, trying to engage a waiter in conversation, lighting up just another cigarette, pretending to be lost in thought, humming old tunes, anything, just sweet anything, so long as not to be forced back into the cold night. A fat pink Frenchman was arguing with a waiter about the quality of champagnes. At another table an old man was sobbing. The band, indicating the jubilee was over again, packed their instruments into their cases with automatic care. A man got up on the floor and began to dance with a broom. The head waiter passed by André shrugging his shoulders significantly. But significantly of what, André thought? And more than anything else the club was just a big empty room. The smart talk of the evening had dissolved, leaving nothing behind – not memory or pain or echo. The music might as well not have been played. The jubilee was for nothing.

An old man hobbled in, fumbling along on a cracked peg-leg. "Good evening, Don André," he said.

André nodded.

The old cripple was one of the sweeper's husbands and held the franchise on cigarette butts.

"Have you a peseta for an old grandfather?"

"I'm sorry. I have nothing on me."

"Ah, don't tell me. I understand. Nightclubs and girls. How I wish I had money to celebrate the *fallas* in such a manner. But I am old and poor. Life has not been kind to me."

André squirmed in his seat.

The old cripple bowed contemptuously. "Ah, yes, it displeases you to see the poor. You are a gentleman and we are so ugly," he said.

"Look! I have nothing."

André pulled out his pockets. Handkerchief, a few *centimos*, two small pencils, a tube of paint. The crumpled hundred dollar bill fell to the floor.

The old cripple stooped down quickly and retrieved the bill. "You dropped this," he said. His beady eyes shone hopefully. "Is this money?"

"It's not mine. It . . ."

The bill lay crumpled on his yellow, shaky hand.

"Yes. It's mine. Take it."

"*Gracias, gracias.*"

He bent over and kissed André's hand with his dry lips.

"Please don't do that."

The old cripple hobbled away.

VII

"Are you sure it's legal?"

"Yes."

"It would be damn embarrassing if I was picked up by the cops, you know. I've got my family to think of."

"It is legal."

"Hell, I wish I had my camera with me. I could probably get some damn fine shots."

"They charge extra to take pictures."

"I don't mean those kinda pictures. I mean pictures! I'm interested in all this from a sociological point of view. I'm making an album of my European tour."

"Would you like to buy some pictures?"

"You mean *real* pictures?"

"Yes."

"Yeah, sure. But later, huh? Let's go."

"First let's have another cognac."

"Sure. I have all you want."

"Pep!"

Pep groaned.

"*Dos cognacs. El Mejor.*"

"Christ, I can't get over how good you speak English."

"I was a sailor. I told you. I was five years in New York."

"Yeah, that's right. You told me. I must be getting drunk."

Luís said nothing.

"You'll stay with me all the time, huh? I don't speak the language. I . . ."

"I will stay with you all the time. You must give me one hundred pesetas."

"Sure. Don't you worry about the money."

"I'm not worried."

"Do they do anything you want? You know what I mean."

"Anything."

"Let's go, huh?"

"Let me finish my drink."

"I'll buy you all you want later. Let's go."

A fog of cigarette fumes drifted about the ante-room. The sweaty walls seemed to shed faded wallpaper like dead skin. Seated atop a high stool, plump Rosita presided over a counter on which were piled orderly stacks of chips. Had Rosita been born a man or of a good family she might have been a tycoon or a politician; as it was, she was sole owner of the *casa*. She twirled the faceless, dirty, copper coins in her hands. Dependent on their size they merited; *una vez, dos veces,* the whole night. She was dressed in a black gown. She had about her the air of the smug showman assured of an unending season and the universality of her attractions. She was human though, Rosita. She had loved, she had suffered. Was there no justice? With all her loot, all her gold, where was she admitted? And ha! she could tell them! she was no worse, not one bit worse, than any of them! And *madre mía* she knew them all. They all came dribbling through her door, their lust-hungry tongues hanging and their eyes popping – so cheap they couldn't talk to a girl without pinching, squeezing, feeling, pawing ... crawling for their copper chips, begging for their quickies or their nights of splendour. And they were all the same – the anarchists and the bankers ... the jerk-off Jesuits and the ac/dc nuns raiding the collection plate for the one-a-month hallelujah go with *pequeña Pepita mía!* ... the workers cheating on their bread money because ah the charms of Pilar! And the pot-bellied bastards! the giggling men-children, saving it up like misers, careful not to lift anything heavy and following a special diet, still good for only one huff-and-puff throw. And she, Rosita (if not for her they would be walking the streets, going for months without a decent examination), not worthy of them?! Oh, the stories she could tell.

Giddy with anger Rosita fingered a copper coin that was worth a full night of uninterrupted lovemaking. She smiled at Barney – properly respectful, properly reserved. Only her lips contradicted her superficial amicability. They were bitter, twisted, knowing.

"Hell, she's a real business man, you know. No funny stuff. I can tell that by just looking at her."

"Yes. She is very shrewd."

"Look – em – frankly, I mean. Do you think any of them are sick? I've got a wife and ...'"

"They are clean."

"Swell."

"Come into the parlour with me."

The parlour was painted pink. It was a huge, unfurnished room. Wooden benches lined the drab walls. The other end of the room led into a long hallway and the bedrooms. Eight or nine men, their faces distorted in various stages of sexual anticipation, lingered restlessly on the benches. They laughed too loudly at each other's jokes, they slapped each other too heartily on the back. An old, pot-bellied man was seated apart from them. His skin was jaundiced, wrinkled. He brought the girls

their pails of hot water and towels when they drifted into the
bedrooms with their lovers. Beside him, on the bench, lay a
basket of sweets. Now and then he shuffled about the room,
insulting and cursing the men until they condescended to buy
their girl a candy. He picked idly at his nose and sneaked glances
at Pilar because her breasts were showing. Pilar despised him.
But there were some things the other men would not do.

"Sweetheart," a young soldier said in a falsetto voice, "how
much to do a little job for me?"

All the men on the bench giggled.

The old man spat over his shoulder. "What a soldier! How
much do you earn a month, boy? Is it enough to spend fifteen
minutes with Pilar? Or do you think you could last that long?"

"Old pimp! Is it true that the girls play games with you
after the house closes down?"

"You talk as if you feel at home here, boy. Perhaps your
mother works here?"

"Say that again!"

"Perhaps your mother works here? Or perhaps she only
drops in to bring your sister sandwiches?"

Two of the other men got up and pushed the soldier back
on the bench.

"Don't be a fool!"

"He's just a filthy old bastard!"

The old man roared with laughter.

The girls, dressed in kimonos or black underwear or sheer
gowns, gossiped noisily in a corner of the room. They sat
around like stuffed animals, absently scratching their thighs.
Their faces were dull and their bodies weary, legs and arms
as impersonal as empty stockings. They were neither sad nor
forlorn – just empty, like dead souls. None was older than
thirty or younger than fourteen. Some of them had been
dancers, others had played bit parts in music halls. Occasionally one of the girls would break away from the group and
spring on to one of the young men's laps, kissing and fiddling

with him. This failing to encourage him she would soon abandon him, slapping him playfully in parting. Soon another girl came along – blonde following brunette, fat following lean, young following old – until the aroused men were forced into selecting a partner. Amid laughter they would make their way to the bedroom.

"They are very young here," Luís said.

"I like the one in the black slit skirt. Hell, she looks like the goods all right!"

"Shall I call her over?"

Barney hesitated. "You're sure they're okay, huh? No clap or anything?"

"I am certain."

"How many times do you think they get it every night?"

"I don't know. It depends."

"There must be at least thirty of them here, huh?"

"Yes."

"She must really clean up!"

"We call her the Queen."

"Why?"

"It's difficult to explain."

"I'll bet it is. This is no place for a queen!"

The girls were gathered around Lolita. She was new, from Cadiz. She had first gone into a brothel in Seville, five years ago, when she had been fourteen. That year, among the tourists in town for Holy Week, there had been a phenomenal demand for virgins. An enterprising pimp had picked her up in the slums of Cadiz and offered her five hundred pesetas to come to Seville. What a girl she had been then! Such a body! (She showed the others a photo.) Now she was weary – always as if she had just finished running a race. She no longer excited men – *Qué lástima, Lolita!* You make love like a dead woman. Isn't my money as good as the next man's? And now she was only able to attract clients by permitting the perversions that had horrified her four years ago. And even then she was only an extra girl, working small towns that lacked for amusements during the off-season.

Spread out on her lap was an album, cheap blurred snaps of the Photomaton variety. Each tawdry photo represented one of her lovers, lovers of a night and sometimes lovers of a month. In her whining, frightened voice she was telling the girls about Ramón. Yes, she agreed with Carmen, he hadn't been as handsome as López or as generous as René, but he had been really funny. And if Jaime had been free and easy with his money hadn't he been the one who had infected her? Yes . . . (slowly, nostalgically, she flipped over the page). Ah, here was Jorge! He came every night for six weeks. Look, the Norwegian! And Julian, who had paid extra so that he might beat her with a belt. But, the Norwegian. Arne, I think, was his name. . . .

Suddenly Valentina kicked up her leg and the album went flying through the air. Photos scattered in all directions, flipping and twisting, slowly spiralling downwards.

Lolita gasped. She turned pale. "Why did you do that? You didn't have to do that."

Pilar snickered. The others remained silent. Valentina was chieftain among the girls. Also, she was Francisco's mistress. It was Francisco who arranged those appointments for the afternoon and those lovely week-ends in the country. It was Francisco who journeyed to Palma for hashish. If one offended Valentina one was liable to be cut off for a week.

"Silly bitch!" Valentina said. "What do we care for your pictures? If you are going to work here you will have to learn not to be proud. Understand?"

Lolita got down on her hands and knees and began to gather up the photos.

A few of the girls laughed grimly.

"Do you think they get any fun out of it?" Barney asked. "It's just a job."

"You know it's okay with a whore if you know what I mean. You can horse around a bit. With your wife it's a different story. I mean a guy feels kind of dirty. Don't you think so?"

"Yes."

A dark girl caught Barney's eye and smiled at him beneath drooping eyelids. Smiling still, she ran her hands down her kimono. She fondled herself not in joy or with a sense of wonder, but as if she understood, as if everyone understood. Slowly she walked towards him.

She sat down beside him, her kimono hanging open.

"*Cómo se llama su amigo?*" she asked Luís.

"No capishe!" Barney said.

"She wants to know your name."

"My name is Jones . . . Henry Jones."

"*Él se llama Enríque.*"

"*Quién es?*"

"*Es un tonto Americano.*"

"What's going on? What did she say?"

"She says you are very handsome."

"Tell her she's okay."

"*Él dice que tu es muy guapa.*"

"*Tío! Claro.*"

Long locks of hair fell down to her shoulders and gathered in silken tangles on her black kimono. The richer black of her hair glistened on the shabby robe like strands of ebony. She sat down on Barney's lap and kissed him. Barney laughed.

"Hey! She's really the goods." Barney kissed her and he was careful not to touch her lips. "Me come. Me you boom-boom!"

She laughed, tickling him under the chin.

"Ask her how much."

Across the room Pilar found herself a lover. The old man, the guardian of the pails and towels, was dozing. The couple crept up on him silently and careful not to awaken him. Then, just as they were upon him, Pilar turned her plump behind on him and broke wind. The old man awakened with a start.

"Ask her how much!"

BOOK THREE

MONDAY

Qué sientes en tu boca
roja y sedienta?
El sabor de los huesos
di mi gran calavera.

F. GARCÍA LORCA

What is it you feel
In your red, thirsty mouth?
The taste of the bones
Of my big skull.

I

IN FRONT OF the *Correos y Telégrafos* building a slim civil guard with grieving black eyes and a tiny black mustache yanked uncomfortably at his gunstrap. Two other guards, shining black submachine-guns strapped to their shoulders, paced to and fro before the building. Then, towering above the crowds, came a slender artillery captain. Quickly the men in grey jerked to attention. Then they slumped again, turning their faces to the crowds wandering about the plaza.

Barney groaned. He cracked his knuckles and he crossed his legs; he uncrossed his legs and he lit a cigarette – impatiently he ground the cigarette to bits with his heel. What kind of fiesta was this, he thought? Fireworks, and fireworks. Three times a day they try and blow your head off! Parades, bands. When were they gonna burn the goddam things? Money for this and money for that. Soon there'll be a special charge for breathing! (This made him laugh.) And the heat! Sonavabitch heat, cost-too-much-money heat, underwear-sticking heat. New Orleans woudiv been more like it, man! All those juicy nigger broads just begging for it! Not Jessie lying ice-cold on a slab (Conchita thought he was fine) waiting till *you're* all puffed out and then turning her motor on.

The mob jamming around him on the terrace of Café Ruzafa was yelling, drunken, and sweating. Was Litri superior to Aparicio? Is it true that Luís Miguel was finished? *Fútbol? Fútbol?* . . . a giant of a man yelled. Who in the hell gives a damn about *fútbol?* Somebody has seen the bulls. *Muy feo!* A novice – *un novicio, hombre!* my five-year-old son could dance around such bulls and kill a hundred in an afternoon. Who has seen Miguel? MIGUEL! The bastard has run off with my tickets! A whore swears she has slept with Manolete. What? With Manolete? This barrel of flesh! Belly laughter, beer laughter. Three times I slept with him! Howling laughter. Did you hear? Ha! She, yes this one. *With Manolete.* Three times! Pinches for her rosy cheeks, pinches for her bum. Gómez shoves a ten-peseta note down her bosom. BRING HER DRINKS! Shall Manolete's mistress die of thirst? Sweat, laughter, joy. She's old enough to have slept with Manolete's father! Scalpers drift in and out among the men selling tickets for the afternoon fights. Old enough to – ho, ho. That was good! Did you hear? Eh? More cognac! MORE COGNAC! Miguel; PEPE! Impossible to walk on the streets. Crowds, *get yourself a table and don't let go.* Boiling sun! Not a cloud, not a cloud. If only it lasts until evening. What? *Litri tiene miedo?* Hey, look – look! A FIGHT! Not today, not today. Cognac for all! That's it, shake hands. MIGUEL! What? You slept with Móntez? What a day! All the great whores of Spain here. For after the fights, for after the drinks. *Cien pesetas para sombre? Vamos, hijo de puta!* Such women. My, my. *Drinks*, DRINKS! *Guapa!* such a lovely ass. What? Come on, fiestas don't last for ever. Gómez! GOMEZ! Did you hear what she asked me? And she stinks so much from sweat. PEPE! Rowdy, happy, crazy. *Camarera! Por favor!* What, fighting again? *Amigos, amigos! No, señor!* IT IS APARICIO WHO IS AFRAID! Separate them! Quick! Have a drink. Have Manolete's mistress! PEPE!

Barney stirred uneasily in his seat. If he could join these men for a drink, if he could share their jokes. No, always he was the outsider. So what! They were just a bunch of nogoods –

he could buy and sell a dozen in an afternoon! Barney got up unsteadily, and pushing his way through the mob, he attempted to cross the street. He got mixed up in a parade and an enormous woman tried to dance with him. Barney swore under his breath, shoved the woman, and managed to break away.

The men were still yelling: GÓMEZ! Pepe!

Barney was sorry he had so much to drink and he was sorry he had been to the brothel. He felt cheap. Knocking against people, falling back again, bumping against others, he finally forced his way across the street. He rubbed the breast pocket of his jacket as if he was brushing away dust and only when he felt the reassuring bulge was he satisfied. Now, suddenly, he discovered that he was standing in front of the Mocambo Club.

The bar was empty. Apparently it was closed. But the bartender – a plump, stocky, grey-haired man, sipping muscatel himself – made no objection when Barney sat down on a stool.

"Cognac," Barney said.

The bartender set a bottle and a glass down on the bar and moved away. He sat down in a chair that was tilted against the wall and began to read a book.

The dark and empty bar frightened Barney.

He poured himself a cognac. His hands were shaking. *She's in love with the Goy André.* Among the crowds it had only been a whisper: now it was a shout. All the things that have happened to me, he thought. Always everybody against me. Maybe if I had had an education, maybe if I had studied law like Louis. But when was there money in the family? When could I have afforded it? And what about Louis? Look at him! Coming around begging for cases – an ambulance-chaser! Always studying, always pulling off those crazy marks in school, always talking his head off about books. Now look at him, earning less than a waiter. *Scholarships!* Married to that

TB Abromovitch girl. Making a jerk out of himself for Wallace. (As if there are no pogroms in Russia; as if anybody, *anybody at all* – all!)

He remembered his happy jobbing days, his struggle. The one-horse towns and the half-assed Ford always breaking down on the road, the meals that were always waiting for him at home on the weekends – *gefilte fish, latkas,* roast chicken, *kreplach.* His mother smiling and crazy, his father always full of questions. (So they were bad to you, the *Goyim?* So they talked behind your back? A black year on them! Hitlers!) And the mad miscellany of goods he had carried – children's toys, flashlights, washable playing cards, combination cigarette-lighter pens, household gadgets, luminous paint. Anything that would make those goddam hicks open up their eyes. The short-order joints in the Bronx. Then, the others, in Brooklyn, Manhattan, Jersey, Yonkers. Business expanding, everything good. Then, finally, the *real* restaurants. Miss Raymond of Garfield-Connelly had been hired to promote the first of the restaurants. (He had known few women. There had been the Delancy Street girls, who were always pulling off the marriage act; and the blondes in the hotels on the road, okay for horsing around with but how did it improve a guy?) Suddenly, here was Miss Raymond! Like the girls he had seen, and having seen, adored, going to church Sunday morning in Utica; like the girls in the *Collier's* stories and *Saturday Evening Post* illustrations. Miss Jessica Raymond of the Jacksonville Raymonds. (Even now it was so clean and good to say. Listen: Jessica Raymond of the Jacksonville Raymonds.) He was going places, he was smart; he was going places where he could not drag a ghetto girl with her singsong and her red red lipstick.

The bartender got up. He poured himself a glass of muscatel, and then refilled Barney's glass. "*Nu? Vos macht a yid?*" Chaim asked, smiling.

"Hey! You're a Jew."

"Yes."

"And you speak English!"

"Why not?"

Chaim was drunk. He was celebrating the *fallas*, he was celebrating André and Toni's romance, he was celebrating the loss of his club. "I'm celebrating today," he said. "Are you celebrating?"

"No."

Barney was embarrassed. Maybe he's working up to a touch, he thought. "Hey, you're a character all right," he said.

"Are you from New York?"

"Yes."

"You know Clinton Street?"

"Yeah."

"The theatre where Rosenberg and his wife play?"

"No. I never had time for Yiddish theatre. My wife likes sophisticated stuff. Broadway."

Barney lit a cigarette. Why does he frighten me? he thought. "Why is the bar so empty?" he asked.

"I'm closed. The bar is changing ownership. I'm out of a job."

Another parade was passing. Barney could hear the drums. He winked at Chaim. "Got any women here, Jakey? You know, I can pay."

"My name is Chaim."

Barney began to fidget with his glass. "Well . . . Chaim?"

"No. I'm afraid not."

Barney felt that Chaim held some sort of advantage over him. He pulled his wallet out. "Would you like to see some snaps of my kids?" he asked.

They'll be ashamed of me, Barney thought.

He handed Chaim the photos. "That's Sheldon here," he said, "and that's Mary Anne. Both bright as hell. And don't ask me which is my favourite because I don't believe in that kind of crap. It's not right for the kids."

"They look very sweet," Chaim said, handing back the photos.

Suddenly Barney felt *this is another Jew*, and he wanted to reach out and grab him. There were so many things they could talk about – pogroms, wars, regimes, prospects, the others, how hard it was. But Barney thought: He would only laugh at me.

"I envy you. I wish I had children."

Barney laughed a quivering laugh. "Never too late, pop. Not if you can still get it up, huh?" He refilled his glass. "Hey, you know my wife is waiting for me now. She always gets nervous if I'm out of her sight for five minutes. Scared I might make off with some other broad." He snapped his fingers. "Phfft! The hell with it! A dime a dozen. The way to hold on to them is to play hard-to-get. Remember that, eh, pop? Say Barney Laz . . . Larkin told you so. But don't go off thinking I don't love the wifey. I'm nuts about her! But you only live once, pop. Isn't that right, huh? Hey, look!" He emptied his wallet. "See all that money? Well, it means sweet nothing to me. Easy come, easy go. That's the trouble with me. You know what's the trouble with me? I'm just too goddam easy with money. Need money, eh? Go see Big Barney Larkin! Everybody says it. So what? So you only live once, huh?"

"Yes," Chaim said, stuffing the bills back into the wallet.

"Hey! Watcha doin?" Barney tossed his head back and tried to take a glass of cognac in one shot. He began to cough.

"Wait," Chaim said. "I'll get some coffee. We'll have a cup together."

"Coffee? Do you think this is all I can handle?"

Chaim remembered Barney. He had seen him, and having seen him felt his heart go sad, a hundred thousand times. What's going to happen, he thought? There are the books, the music, the ideas; but what's to be done for Barney? The Guillermos hate him; the Andrés avoid him; I am too old. But Barney goes on, and on, and on. He hates the Cossacks; and one day he hopes to dine with their generals. Barney, Barney, Barney.

"No, of course not," Chaim said. "But I'm not as young as you are. I'm feeling a bit . . ." Chaim reached out and placed his hand on Barney's. "What is it?" he asked.

Barney snatched his hand away quickly. "Hey, look! Waddiya take me for?"

Chaim flushed. "Yes," he said. "I'm getting old. This job doesn't pay very much. It's difficult to be a Jew in a foreign country. I imagine it must be the same in America. But you must be very successful and they wouldn't dare bother you. I'm saving up to go to Israel. Our land! A place where a Jew can go if he's in trouble and be sure to find friends. Love, too, if that's what he needs. Especially if he feels he wants to begin his life over again with new ideas. That's the way I feel, you know. But I wish I had children to take with me! Or that I was a successful man with something to contribute. Do you think I'm right? I'd like your advice."

Barney felt his hand sting where Chaim had touched him. He laughed, and slapped the bar. "Sure, pop," he said. "Told dozens of people the same thing. Go somewhere where you belong. Build up the country. Sometimes when I think of the possibilities I wouldn't mind getting in on new territory myself, but it would mean giving up so much. I'm all for it, though. Give them loads of cash every year. Hey, it's ten o'clock. Gotta run, pop. The wifey! Sure glad to have met you. Here, take this fiver. Have another one. Sure, go ahead. It'll keep you in cigarettes on the boat. So long. And look, don't worry. You'll make out swell."

Chaim watched him go, stumbling up the steps leading to the street. He felt sad, guilty also. He stared down at the two five-dollar bills. He thought: I was wrong to fool with him that way. But there is no idea or cause that will save us all. Salvation is personal.

Yes, Barney knew, drinking was their way. But if that's how she wanted him, he would show her. A nogood like André wasn't going to ruin their marriage. He paused in front of the hotel, rocking to and fro on his legs. Old Carlos watched from his shop window, a silky grin on his face. Goddam jerk, Barney thought. Serve him right if I popped into his joint and smacked him one on the jaw. He visualised the scene as if it was happening in a movie. Old Carlos the fence, knocked down and bleeding among the smashed flowerpots, and he, good old Barney Bogart, telling the amazed cops that it was really nothing, just nothing at all boys.

With difficulty Barney read the sign on the window.

> *On parle Français*
> *Sprechen Duetsch*
> *English spoke*

Carlos smiled enticingly at him. He was short and dark and he stank of *eau de cologne* and cognac. His dyed black hair was greased down to his oblong skull like a shining plate of metal.

Barney entered the shop.

"*Oui, Monsieur?*"

"Not French," Barney said gruffly, emphasising his masculinity. "American."

Old Carlos rubbed his long elegant fingers together. "Ah, American! A democrat. You have such beautiful handsome sailors. They were only here last month, such brave . . ."

"I want a hundred pesetas worth of flowers!"

"*Si, si, si.*" Carlos bowed, dipping forward from the waist. "But what kind of flowers?"

"What do I know about flowers? Gimme a hundred pesetas worth of the best!"

"*Oui, Monsieur.*"

"And – em – hold on a second! All kinds of colours, huh?"

Carlos bowed again. "Oh, *Monsieur*, you do not know what a pleasure it is to serve someone from your great country. We Spaniards you know suffer greatly under Franco. Oooh, it is terrible. Very, most, terrible. We had such a bloody revolution and so many beautiful young men were killed. Brother against brother, boys with guns on the street."

"Are you a Red?"

Carlos gathered up an assortment of roses and geraniums and daffodils. "*Monsieur, s'il vous plaît!*" He paused, a dapper fencer holding a shield of flowers before him. "I am a Monarchist. My mother was presented to Don Alfonso the …"

"Okay, fine." Barney wiped the sweat off his forehead. "But royalty don't impress us Americans. You might as well learn that. We like people to be free."

"One hundred and fifty pesetas."

"I only wanted to spend …"

"But *Monsieur* asked for flowers of the best quality!"

Barney handed him a five-hundred peseta note. "I'm in a hurry," he said.

Old Carlos drifted over to a pot of red roses and rearranged them in a perfunctory manner. He handed Barney his change. "And if *Monsieur* has any American dollars he would like to have changed?"

Vividly Barney recalled all the gory tales of homosexual passion he had read in *The Sunday News*. I wonder if I should report him, he thought. "No," he said. "No money to change."

Carlos bowed.

Tottering, just a bit unsure of himself, Barney pushed open the door to their room. Jessie was not in.

II

"Do you know what I want now?" he asked.

"What, my lover?"

"Breakfast in bed."

His arm still embracing her naked shoulder, his hand soft on her, their legs tangling underneath the blankets. They lay calm. Her head, round and small and black, firm against his chest. Her hand caressing lazily – now upwards from his belly, passing, learning every bump and fall in his body; then, downwards from his eyes, pressing against his throat, sliding downwards on his chest, stopping now for a pinch or to commit to memory.

He smiled. She covered his smile with her hand, holding it and then feeling it disappear. "I had to cover you up three times last night," she said. "When you fell asleep I was lonely."

"I'm sorry."

She was leaning over him, her breasts dipping and full. He yanked at her black hair. "Stop frowning!" he said.

Still, her eyes were full of concern.

"I love you so much." And she added to herself, sorrowfully: But you will never love me, never. I am a project for you.

He laughed.

Sleep-smell filled the room with warmth.

"I want breakfast in bed every morning!"

"Oh!" she gasped, faking fright.

"Well?"

"Starting tomorrow."

"Starting today!"

She rolled over on to his belly, and bit his neck. He caught her in his arms, pushing her away gently. He forced her back on the bed, then leaning over her he rolled his head on her breasts, showering hot quick kisses on her. Then they both lay back again, she against his shoulder, black hair falling on him.

"Did you fight Colonel Kraus because he kissed me?" she asked.

I am in bed with a woman, he thought. Her sweat is drying on my body.

"I've done many bad things. Sometimes I hit people to make up for it."

"Sometimes when you're jealous you frighten me."

"Toni, promise me you won't see him again."

"It's difficult. If he comes into the club . . ."

"Then that you won't dance with him. Or talk to him."

She kissed his swollen cheek. "I promise," she said. "Do you know what I want?"

"What?"

"Guess."

"A bucket of sun to wash your hair in?"

"No."

"A purple tree for our bedroom?"

"No."

"Two golden stars to paste on your breasts?"

"No, no, no."

"I give up."

"I give up, *darling!*"

"I give up, darling, darling."

She shouted in his ear. "I want a cigarette!"

"But darling," he said, "that's the way it all starts. With the first cigarette. And you are so young."

Underneath the blankets, she slapped him.

"Oh, you bitch!"

"Do I get my cigarette?"

He sat up in bed. Lanky, nervously thin. Sharp sunlight poured into the room and chiselled out yellowed patterns on the blankets. The roar and rush of a world that was no longer theirs rattled on the window. He passed his hand through a shaft of sunlight and began to turn it over thoughtfully. He wiggled his slender fingers; then, turning his hand, palm upwards, he tried to cup the light in his hand. We don't ask much, he thought. Just some time, some love, and a room.

"I want a cigarette."

"Where did I go wrong, Toni?"

"Wrong?"

"I am a coward."

Inside St. Peter's, standing underneath the dome, he had slowly begun to look upwards. Searching for the top of the dome, he had suddenly realised that his neck was craned backwards as far as it would go, and he lost his balance. Guillermo left him with the same feeling. "I don't think I really like Guillermo," he said.

"Oh, but I do want a cigarette, darling!"

He picked up the package from where he had left it on the floor and lit two cigarettes. Then he held the match to her lips and she blew it out. He lay back on the pillow and sighed effortlessly. She turned on her side, leaning over him. Her black hair fell on his shoulders.

"I love your eyes most of all."

"I'm afraid you are not very handsome."

"I have character."

"Only old men have character."

They kissed.

"Tell me about the olive trees."

"Oh, darling!"

"I love when you tell me about the olive trees. Or the island."

Toni laughed, but her voice was solemn. "The olive trees are more than a thousand years old. My father said they were planted by the Phoenicians. The trees are all in agony, none of them stand erect. They are all knees and knuckles: each trunk is gnarled like a corkscrew. The legend says Holy Men passed by five hundred years ago and twisted each deformed trunk until the sap refused to drip any longer. But when there is a death on the island the trees drip again. If one has not sinned one can find drops of blood around the trunks. The trees are human, and their shrug is the posture of the old.

They will go on reaching heavenwards with mangled hands until He comes down to us again."

"They must be wonderful trees."

"Sometimes when there is a storm at sea the women lay flowers underneath the trees. But the priests are furious when they find out. So the women must go out at night, and in secret." Toni frowned. "You got up twice last night to smoke."

"Yes."

"Why?"

"So I could watch you sleep."

"No, please, darling. Why?"

"I was thinking. Sometimes I get crazy ideas."

He pulled himself upwards for an instant, kissing her chin.

"What were you thinking about last night?"

Puffs of smoke curled upwards to the ceiling.

"Not now."

"André . . . will you want me to have children?"

"Yes. But not for a long time."

"Why? Why don't we have a child now?"

"You're not pregnant, are you?"

"No. Of course not."

"Toni . . . ?"

"No, of course not. Don't be silly!"

He tried to blow a smoke ring. It was not very good.

"This is lovely, Toni. It makes everything else seem so foolish. It isn't quite fair."

"Was she pretty, André?"

"Who?"

"Ida."

"Ida?"

"You often call out her name in your sleep."

He sat up, swinging his legs over the edge of the bed.

"She was very pretty. She was foolish and happy and pretty. Her eyes were sad and without end. Even when she laughed her eyes were sad."

"How did you meet her?"

"At a party. Let's not talk about it, Toni."

"No, I want to know."

"Let's go for a walk."

"You were at the university then, weren't you?"

"Yes."

"Tell me about the university."

"The university?" He laughed unconvincingly. His face was drawn. "It was just a university. The girls read Freud and the boys pretended to be revolutionaries. Oh, hell, I don't want to talk about it."

"You were very unhappy at the university."

"Yes. I was snubbed by the campus intellectuals because my name was Bennett and that implied a hell of a lot. I rented a luxurious apartment near the university. I gave fabulous entertainments in my rooms. Everyone used to make wise-cracks about me. Bennett of the New Aristocracy. Comrade Moneybags Bennett. The football-cocktail set ignored me because I refused a fraternity key. Also, my father's huge industrial empire outdid the collective financial achievement of all their families combined. I tried to get some attention by holding an exhibition in the Student's Union. I was shut down the first afternoon because of the 'obscene' content of my work. Whatever company I had I paid for by diving for the bill wherever I went. That's all. It isn't very interesting."

"And Ida, did she ignore you?"

He lay back on the bed.

The ceiling was cracked in places. The plaster was dirty.

"When I met her she was just in the process of escaping from a very restricted home. Ida was president of a silly group called the Skeptics Club, and she used to write neurotic letters to the college paper saying that Hitler hadn't killed off the Jews fast enough, or that the only way to settle population problems was to drop atom bombs on China and India every spring. She was truly wonderful, but most of the students were afraid of her. When the communists invited a negro unionist to speak at one of their student meetings Ida was appointed to introduce him. She showed up in black-face and was promptly thrown out. What did it all matter? We were students. We could go to the movies or sit in a bar all afternoon.

"I met her and I fell in love with her. It was at one of my parties. She got very drunk and she insisted that I do a pornographic painting of her. Christ, I could have finished the damn thing in a week but I was afraid that she would leave me! Secretly I was pleased that she was a Jewess and notorious. I would marry her and that would show everyone. My family, the intellectuals, the leftist clubs, the fraternities. It would be a sensation!"

He got out of bed and walked over to the sink. He turned on the cold water tap and let it run. He had the odd sensation of everything – yet nothing in particular – in his body tingling. He wanted to shout or rip himself apart.

"When did you find out that she was pregnant?"

"Chaim tell you?"

"No, not exactly."

"Did he tell you how much my father paid for it? He did, you know. Great guy, my pop. He even offered to pay my fare to Europe. Son, he said, in the next war I'll get you a commission. I hope you'll be lucky enough to get killed."

He poured himself a glass of water, took a sip, then emptied the glass in the sink.

"Come back into bed darling. Lie down beside me. Tell me the rest."

He lay back on the bed again and stared at the cracks in the ceiling. She kissed him on the chest. She ran her hand through his hair.

"When she told me I offered to marry her on the spot. I never expected her to be anything but delighted. After all, even if I was such a fine socialist I was still André Bennett of the Canadian Bennetts. And who was she? Just a frivolous little Jewess born of Polish immigrant parents. But the prospects of my proposal seemed to alter her completely. I begged, I pleaded. No, she said. It's impossible. Her parents wouldn't hear of it! They would die of grief! They were old, and she was all they had. She said she knew of a doctor and would I lend her the money. I gave her a blank cheque. She told her parents she was going to the Laurentians with friends. They wouldn't suspect anything. She wouldn't allow me to come with her or even investigate the doctor. All I had to offer her was money! She said she would write. She would see me within a week. I let her go! I was even relieved, proud. I was twenty years old and already a reckless lover! Two weeks passed and I heard nothing. I decided to visit her family."

He lit a cigarette off an old butt. Toni held her fingers to his lips. She believed, this way, she could absorb some of his anguish. She listened to the sound of his voice more than to the meaning of his words. For the melancholy pitch of his voice – the names pronounced with such hesitation and the words that came so hard and cruel from his lips – told her far more than he was admitting as the truth.

"It was Friday night and I was drunk. They lived in a foul-smelling St. Dominic Street flat in the heart of the Montreal ghetto. I'll never forget the look in the old woman's eyes when she saw me come in. She knew who I was without asking. She showed me into the parlour. Old Mr. Blumberg was seated at the supper table reading from a prayer book by candlelight. He was old and wizened, he rocked to and fro as he read. He had long sidecurls which made him look very sorrowful and he wore a square skullcap. He scrutinised me for an instant without saying anything. Suddenly he began to weep. It wasn't the sound of a man crying or even of an animal. He looked up at me as if he was afraid that I might whip him. Why did you have to do it? he said. Why can't you leave us alone? Haven't you had enough amusement with us? Will you always murder us for your enjoyment? Will you rape my old wife now? Isn't it enough that you have murdered our Ida? I was terrified! I picked him up bodily from the chair and began to shake him. She isn't dead! She isn't dead, I said. I love her. Why don't you let me marry her? Behind me his wife was shrieking for the neighbours. She is dead, he said. She died with your filth inside her. Now will you go? Now will you leave us? Murderer! I couldn't help it. I just couldn't help it! I hit him. You don't know how an old man can look at you, how . . . She wouldn't even let me help him up. The neighbours rushed in. And together, they threw me out.

"All I wanted was for her death to have some dignity. Was it too much to ask? Why did they all have to take it up and make her a cause?

"I sold all my belongings and I came to Europe. Wasn't that noble of me? Isn't that just great?"

He got up. He paced about the floor as if he did not know where to throw his naked body, as if he was seeking a place where he could break it, end it, and where it might remain hidden so others could not come and look at his shame.

He tried to open the window but the bolt was jammed. He smashed his fist down on it again and again but nothing gave way. Toni rushed up from behind and embraced him, pressing her cheek against his hot and naked back. He could feel that behind him, she was also naked. Then he saw him, down there below the window, Kraus looking up at him.

"André! What is it?"

He smashed his fist through the window. Glass tumbled to the street, and in an instant they heard the crash.

She grabbed his bloody fist and held it to her lips.

"André," she began, her voice full of endearment.

His eyes, now that he looked at her, were oddly calm.

III

Coming slowly up towards him on the Calle de Ruzafa amid the shrinking shadows of noon a parade of men toppled over each other gleefully. Hats awry and shirt tails hanging, thumping away merry and raucous on homemade drums, they snaked their tipsy way up the street holding high placards booming the arrival of the bullfighters to Valencia. Gangs of children followed after them, wagging their tongues at the drummers, yelling and cheering.

... and he would with his money and power, and he would organise an army of golden knights and charge up from the Puerta del Sol plucking fat Franco from his throne, installing by popular demand perhaps even himself the president of a democratic Spain, not anarchist or communist Spain (didn't they detest him simply because he was a gentleman?), but a free *caballero's* Spain, where the lovely women of Castile might enchant the streets of evening unmolested, where the knights in gold such as himself might woo them among the blossoming almond trees, underneath the palms of spring, on the beds of the vineyards of hot La Mancha. ...

And now shadows wilting and sun hot and watchful, desperately drunk paraders, drumsticks booming on canvas as taut and hollow as their stomachs, tumbled past Juanito.

... and one day soon I shall climb into my golden armour and mount my white charger and shout down to the soldiers even now waiting in the square – *Y ahora a luchar!*

In the very spring of time I stand on the balcony of the *Palacio Nacional*, roses and daffodils and sunflowers fall from the sky, I am surrounded by ministers and mistresses, below yelling mobs swarm further than the eye can see, I spread out my golden arms, there is deep silence. ...

"I refuse the crown. *Viva la República!*"

Mad, wild cheers.

"*Viva el nuevo Cid! Viva Juanito!*"

"*Arriba Don Juanito! Arriba el Libertador!*"

Still unseeing, dreaming drugging exploits, he found himself an unoccupied table on the terrace of Café Ruzafa. Drowsy tourists idled in the shade soaking themselves in lemonade and iced cognacs. The women fanning themselves with the morning paper; the men throwing up an exhaust of cigar smoke and ogling the prostitutes and actresses who were seated cool and slim at other tables.

Sweating, the tourists felt the gas and acids contained in their bellies. And in their mouths were yellow teeth and stuck bits of meat; an awareness of small deaths, many of them, rotting their bodies bit by bit.

"Well, if it isn't the con man from Madrid?"

Juanito didn't immediately recognise him – the weak, dimpled face, the raging drunken eyes.

"Invite me to sit down and I'll tell you how to make Jessie."

Juanito grimaced. Pop went his afternoon daydream; again there was only reality. André was right. Pimp, thief.

"Please sit down, *Señor* . . ."

"Derek."

"*Señor* Derek."

Derek sat down and ordered two sweetened gins. He grinned roguishly. But the heat was in him as well as the others, and he thought: There are people younger than I am. "Are you surprised that I saw you kiss my sister?" he asked.

A man collapsed on the kerb. He sat down, leaning against a lamp post. His eyes were dead, and he had a face like a monkey. He pulled out his handkerchief and, mopping his chest, looked up sadly at Juanito. "It is so hot," he said. Juanito ignored him. "I do not know what to do," the man said.

The street was not as crowded as it had been the previous day. It seemed smaller, grotesque and shrivelled. The people passed by morosely. There were the civil guards, all black and all leather, strolling past; the middle-aged couples searching for tables and walking dreadfully slow; there were the wild youths dancing past; and there were the parading workers full of angry memories, enjoying what for them was a fantastic freedom – the right to march down a street after a band.

"It is so hot," the man on the kerb said. "It is mad."

Juanito scowled. He turned to Derek. "I beg your pardon?" he said.

"Oh, not at all, *amigo*. Do you think I was paying any attention to that slut I was dancing with? My, my. I was watching you in the booth, *amigo*. And guess what else I saw, *Señor* Don Juan. Do you mind if I call you Don Juan?"

Sweat streamed down Juanito's face.

"What did you see?"

"Guess, Don Juan."

"What kind of nonsense is this?"

"Would you like a hint?"

The monkeyish man got up and staggered over to their table. He leaned towards Derek, swaying, and Derek could feel his sour breath on him. The man's hands, like withered twigs, were flat on the table. "I was in the war," he said.

"*Vamos, hombre!*" Juanito said. He turned to Derek. "He is drunk."

The man seized Derek by the shoulders. "My son is in Toulouse. He sells lottery tickets."

"Waiter!"

The waiter hurried over and without expression he shoved the man on to the street. The man, tears rolling down his cheeks and mingling with his sweat, doubled over in a paroxysm of laughter. Suddenly, he got down on all fours. "Look," he cried between laughter. "Woof! Woof!" He scampered over to a group of standing men. Settling on one of them, he began to lick his shoes. "Woof! Grrr!" The man pulled his foot away. But one of the others in the group, a man with rimless glasses, tossed him a coin. "Grr! Woof!" The crowd on the terrace laughed nervously. Several of the prostitutes ordered the men seated with them to toss him coins. Quickly, he was greeted with a shower of coins. Panting, woofing, he gathered them up hastily. Suddenly, he stood up. He spit in Derek's direction; then ran off.

"It begins with M," Derek said.

"Please, Mr. Derek, I beg of you . . ."

"Money, Don Juan." Derek giggled, and took a sip of his gin. "Two hundred dollars' worth. Money! M-O-N-E-Y."

"Please, not so loud."

"Don't worry. I wish you had taken the bastard for the whole roll."

"But I gave the money to André to return to you."

"Did you, D.J.? Well he kept the money for himself and left you with nothing."

"He wouldn't do that. We are great friends. I will speak to him."

"Will you have another gin?"

"No. I don't think so."

"I'm inviting you to another gin, D.J."

"Yes. I am sorry. Very good. . . . Thank you."

"Don't fret, D.J. I'm the only one who knows about it."

Drearily the waiter set two more gins down on the table. A fly had settled on his cheek. He did nothing about it.

Juanito smiled suavely. "I am a fatalist," he said.

And trying to deny the adoration he felt for Juanito's dark body, Derek felt his fingers tingle with an anxiety to touch the other man's lips. Vividly he recalled the scene and the agony which he transported forever with him like a cross – the gorgeous boy from Memphis languishing on the army cot next to him, himself gone weeks without sleep and bursting from denial, leaning over, tenderly, gently, kissing those young lips. Then the betrayal, the beating rendered by the boy that was the very stuff of their love, the shame and humiliation. "Well,

D.J., tell me something about yourself," Derek said. "Is fatalism your philosophy?"

Juanito laughed. "When I die, all I want to leave behind me are my debts."

Derek giggled. He's going to be coy, he thought. All the time he is going to pretend he doesn't understand what was going on.

"I have seen many movies about your country."

"Movies! If any of those Hollywood beautifuls ever saw a Moor close up he would run so fast you couldn't catch him in this world. All of them are pæderasts. Why do you think they have to adopt babies after they get married? Why do you think their women divorce them after two months."

"Still," Juanito said uneasily, "I would like to visit America one day."

"So would every other petty-bourgeois. The democracy of the philistines is reaching its logical conclusion. A kind of sugar-coated fascism doled out by mediocrity. But the tyranny of the proletariat will exceed the boorishness of the petty-bourgeois. The hunger is older, there are more accounts to be settled. I'll tell you what, D.J. Enjoy yourself madly, because pretty soon the hillbillies are going to storm the Winter Palace. Afterwards, darkness."

"Were you in the war?"

"Yes. I was in the war from the beginning."

The old woman, who on other days used to hawk rosaries and crucifixes in the Puerta del Sol, suddenly sold hammer-and-sickle badges and red-and-black anarchist caps. Madrid shall be the Tomb of Fascism, the banners had said. One afternoon, an afternoon when the air-raids were still a joke, he had held hands with Eric in the cinema, watching Fred Astaire and Ginger Rogers in *Gay Divorcee*. That night they had returned to the front by street car. At six a.m. Eric's leg had been shot off, and Derek had watched as he scrambled after it and threw it away.

Juanito noticed a big, somnolent figure detach himself from the strollers-by. Colonel Kraus was not sweating, his walk was brisk, and he hardly seemed to feel the heat or what a fine figure he cut among the exhausted crowd. Kraus nodded at Juanito. "Good afternoon," he said.

"Please sit down, Colonel. Join my American friend and myself for a drink."

Kraus sat down. He turned his rheumy eyes on Derek, mockery and doubt curdling on his doughy face. His English was hard. "I have been to your country," he said. "I was in New York in 1928. I was introduced to Henry Ford. We had dinner together."

"Colonel Kraus has been in the Olympics three times. Once as captain of the German team," Juanito said. He turned to Kraus, smiling.

"Do you know the Canadian?" Kraus asked.

And there was the old unerring military sharpness in his voice. For he was rediscovering himself, even as if the drums were booming again, the voices singing again, throbbing again in his ears, finding himself after six years of slipshod living, sleepy living, rediscovering himself because here again in the shape of André was the enemy. And Kraus knew, just as André knew, what would have to come. The moment under the window had been a moment of recognition.

"The Canadian?" Juanito no longer felt inferior to André. The fact of his theft had endeared him to Juanito. "André?" he said, as if André was not a man but a restaurant vaguely recommended. "You mean the artist? The boy from Montreal?"

Derek giggled inanely. He did not know Kraus but he knew his history. Eric had spoken of him, so had Kleber, so had Gus. Afterwards, Kraus had been briefly at Maidanek where his sister was engaged at the *Vernichtungslager*. Indirectly, she had been connected with the crematoriums. She had been in charge of the checking and stamping of the dead for gold teeth, overlooked rings, and so on. Derek was drunk, and

Kraus frightened him. In the old days I would have been angry, he thought. "If you ask me André is a queer," he said. "Queer as a goat."

"He is just a silly boy, Colonel," Juanito said. "He pretends to come from a good family but . . . Well, there is no explaining the old Jew's likes and dislikes. Perhaps he hopes the paintings will be of some value later on."

Chaim is finished, Kraus thought. I will see about the boy too. "Does the girl love him?" he asked.

"The girl," Juanito said disparagingly. "How can one account for the passing whims of such a child? Perhaps at one time . . . But surely Colonel, you are not interested in such a child. There are many more attractive girls at the club. I would gladly undertake . . ."

"That is enough!" Kraus turned to Derek. "Does Spain please you?"

Derek, who was pale now, smiled. "I have been here before," he said. "In fact, Colonel, I was at Quatro Caminos. You know, on the other side of the Manzanares."

Kraus did not seem to hear. In fact, he had already prepared what he was going to say. "You must pay no attention to what the street Arabs have to say about Franco. There are many malcontents about." Kraus frowned. "You do not know what the Reds did here during the War of Liberation. What they would do again if they had the opportunity. I remember, very well, the campaign around Bilbao.

"I was a captain then. We had just taken a small village near the city. The Reds had fled several hours previous and as usual they had set fire to the whole village. A thirteen-year-old girl had been crucified on the church door. Her stomach had been slit open. Just as we were unpinning the poor child a drunken old man hobbled out of a cave. I forced him to kiss the feet of the murdered child. Now, I said, cry *Viva Franco*. He refused. One of my comrades kicked the old man in the stomach. The old drunk fell on his knees and begged for mercy. I pushed my pistol to his forehead, and said, now! cry *Viva Franco*. He refused. I shot him.

"Everywhere we went we came across murdered priests and raped nuns. The Reds were mad dogs, and we had to shoot them. It was the only way to clean up the country."

Derek stared coldly at Kraus. He remembered the damp nights, the comedy of a handful of *chatos* pitched against the Stukas and Capronis, and he remembered the noble men and the fine songs and the *Salud! Compañeros*. And he realised now and for ever that those days at the front constituted the only moment of truth he had known (not the ideas or the lies or the speeches or the poems or the machines, but the men all together and angry and beautiful). Derek, you are dead: *morte: kaput. You are Judas, and you have been gypped out of your gold.* Derek smiled, Derek laughed. "It's all right, Colonel," he said. "We are allies now. We're all in it together now, but we are screwed. For in the end, that very last battle, will be theirs." And then mentally, to himself, he added: God pity us. And he said: "I was only joking, Colonel. We'll be okay. They haven't got a chance."

Kraus wrinkled up his brow. "Were you in the war?" he asked.

"Yes, I was in the war." And he stood up, pale and shivering and giggling, clutching the crotch of his pants in his fist. "I was wounded three times. The last time – Here!"

Then uncorked misery wringing his face, his raving soul unzipped, naked, he collapsed in his chair, whimpering.

Juanito shrugged his shoulders. "I think he is drunk."

"He is filthy!" Kraus said.

IV

It was time for the afternoon *siesta*.

The sky was hot and cloudless and moist. The trees along the *paseos* drooped in the heat and the flowers in the *plazas* and gardens were wilted and forlorn.

There had been no rain for ten days.

A parade of soldiers erect and proud came marching down the Calle San Vincente. Black boots hit the pavement all together, coming up again in unison; trumpets blew. A young captain, unsmiling, led the band down the street. His drawn sword glittered in the sun.

The band passed, leaving behind it a beating echo; and from her window Fräulein Kraus watched. She drew the curtains quickly. He is only a barman, she thought. It would not do for him to see me watching by the window. She cracked her knuckles; and in her belly she felt the fluttering again. What am I coming to? What am I coming to? What if Roger finds him here and guesses?

I won't answer the door. I will pretend I am out.

She turned away from the window and stopped short in front of the mirror. She smoothed out her black dress and remembered her mother's injunction: after a certain age there was only one colour for a woman, and that colour was black. Alfred, who was dead, had thought differently. He had liked bright colours.

And he had liked laughter.

He had laughed when she had told him that she had informed about the meeting and that there would be many men with lead pipes and gas bombs. Saying: "You found me with Martha so you are jealous. But you would not inform. You are too good for that." Still laughing when he had gone off to Spain carrying freshly won scars, burnt gums and small perforations on his thighs. A Star of David burnt into his flesh although he had been the son of a pastor.

The shades were drawn. There were flowers and a bottle of cognac on the table. The bureau which was in need of repair was in the bedroom.

What does it matter, she thought?

She laughed. Her eyebrows hurt where she had plucked them. Suddenly, not understanding, she held her head in her hands. There was a lump in her throat.

When her weakness finally subsided she walked over to the window again, peeking out from behind the shade. What if I gave him the wrong address, she thought? What if . . .

She walked up and down the room. She rearranged the chairs and straightened out the tablecloth. She wrung her hands. Then, when she thought that she could stand it no longer, he knocked at the door. She opened the door and smiled at him. "It is so kind of you to come," she said.

Luís nodded. There was a somnolent look in his eyes and his body seemed relaxed and powerful. He stepped into the parlour. "Where is the bureau?" he asked. "I must be back at work soon."

She laughed. "There is no hurry. Won't you sit down first?"

Before he could protest she had poured him a glass of cognac. "It is so hot," she said. "But you are so strong. Perhaps you don't feel it as a woman does?"

Suddenly, Luís was embarrassed. He realised that he was angry with her only because she was ugly. If she had been younger or more attractive he would not have minded. He felt restless and unsure of himself. "I think I'd better look at the bureau," he said.

She got up. "It is in the bedroom," she said.

She had lost her way in the winding streets behind the Plaza del Mercado and there the heat had a special smell to it.

The heat smelled of rancid food, children with soiled underwear, uncovered garbage, venereal diseases, sweat and boils, pimpled adolescents with one leg and a stump for another, remedies exchanged across washing-lines, cheats, cross-eyed whores, dirty persons, and no privacy.

Jessie inhaled the stink of the poor which was the stink of her grandfather from Ireland and she felt sick.

Where am I going and why?

What if I divorce him?

No.

But I shouldn't have thrown him out I guess.

The heat was in the sidewalks and in the buildings and she felt it possessing her body. The heat was in the foreign eyes gloomily staring, in the children who paused at their games as she passed in her high-heeled shoes by I. Miller, the heat was a tightening belt around her stomach, it was in the eyes of the housewives lowering their voices when she passed, on the lips of the men exchanging obscenities as she passed. The heat was in her as she tip-tapped by; a long-legged American woman – and she wanted to scream.

Two sullen young men were following her.

In the past, whenever she was faced with a crisis, her father had appeared to her in a dream and told her what to do. But last night she had slept uneasily and there had been no dreams. Somehow the notion of André appealed to her. They were of the same kind, and he could help her. He had such lovely hands, and a kind of gentleness about his mouth. But who knew where he lived?

She stopped to look into a window and the two sullen young men stopped beside her. Jessie felt that she was going to faint, but she knew she mustn't. One of the young men, nonchalantly, moved around to her other side. As he passed she caught a sour whiff of his sweat. He doesn't wash his feet, she thought. The man made an obscene gesture with his hands. His fingernails were dirty.

Suddenly Jessie flung her handbag at him and fled down the street.

The man stared after her, open-mouthed. He turned to his friend, and said: "She had such lovely legs."

"Yes," the other man said.

They reached down for the bag and it felt warm and feminine in their hands. One of the young men, the one who had said she had such lovely legs, held the bag to his cheek.

v

He was envying André for being young and in love and pitying himself for having reached an age when desire was incongruous and sensuality a smutty story. He looked at him and he saw a face that was angry and immature, different from the others only because of the eyes, eyes not American but Slavic or Jewish, eyes mirroring a soul that did tightrope dances on high and windy places.

"Before Christ there were two great teachers among the Jews. Hillel and Shamai. One man was compounded of love and the other only of justice. A Gentile once came to Shamai and said I want to be a Jew. But I am a tailor and I work long hours to earn my living. Teach me to be a Jew on one foot. Shamai was shocked. To be instructed in the great teachings of the Jews in one sitting! He threw the man out of his house. The tailor visited Hillel and repeated his request. Hillel said I shall teach you to be a Jew in one sitting. Do unto your neighbour as you would like your neighbour to do unto you; and you shall be a Jew. And the tailor was proselytised.

"Most evils originate in ignorance, which is a lack of wisdom. And, tell me, what is an ignorant man? An ignorant man is he who believes the whole universe exists only for him. As if nothing else required any consideration."

There was a quality of coolness in the air now.

The sea churned, heaved, gasped – arms of water flinging themselves heavenwards, falling downwards gloomily. Suddenly a star like a pinprick on a faded blue canvas flickered full of hope in the abandoned sky. Far away, just where the sun fell into the sea, the sea yawned, drowning the sun.

"But I like you André because you are not bored. You are not intellectual and uncommitted. You are always taking part, even if not always intelligently. The earth is in your hands and you are dirty."

Swaggering sea rolled tiny fishing smacks to and fro on its exultant thighs. The tangy stink of seaweed, dead fish, rust, invigorated the breezy air. The resounding roar of the sea, the dying sun captured just now in the sails of the smaller fishing craft, the loud lapping of the waves against the boats, impudent prows jerking upwards then flatly falling, grey gulls swooping down into the foam hungrily, all this traffic was as a song of faith beside the anguish of the unending walk of the unemployed, the stunned men who wandered along the docks with less purpose and no more dignified way of obtaining food than wharf rats.

They were seated in front of Cosmi's small café on the waterfront. Chaim leaned back in his chair puffing on a cigar and sipping muscatel. André, seated opposite him, was pale and restless. He scratched his head and puffed anxiously at his cigarette.

"Jesus, Chaim! What are you going to do? It took you years to build up the Mocambo. How will you get a job? What will you do for money?"

"Three years to be exact," Chaim said.

"Okay!" André said quickly. "So you're three years older now."

Chaim chuckled. I should have a family, he thought. Kids to comfort me and spend my money when I'm too old myself. I could have a rabbi, a drunkard, a sweet little nympho daughter all for myself, and a skinny jerk with a *yiddish kop*, somebody serious, who could make money so that the rest of us could enjoy ourselves. "Perhaps I should go to Israel and go into politics?" he said. "I could make a few speeches about the rotten *Goyim* and maybe get a monument put up in my honour? But those communal farms – Riverside Drive Reds wiping their feet on your towel. You come with me, André. We'll start a kind of S.P.C.A. to protect the Arabs."

André shrugged his shoulders.

He and Toni had devoted most of the morning to plan-making. They would go to Paris, and he would give an exhibition; Toni would get a job dancing in a small club; later, as soon as they could afford it, they would rent a small place in Provence. After he had left her he had gone down to the Mocambo to consult Chaim. Luís, who had been watching for him, stopped him at the corner.

"Look, don't worry about me. I told you a hundred times. It's easy to make money. It's the easiest thing in the world. Painting is hard. Being a man is hard. Money? Balls!"

Several flies settled on a puddle of cognac on the table. Quickly, André shooed them away. "I'd fight it," André said. "I wouldn't show so goddam much discretion."

"If I hang around they can put me away for the rest of my life for being here illegally. Let them have the club. I'm tired of it anyway. It was very good of Maríano to tip me off."

"Who in the hell could have told them?"

"I don't know," Chaim said. "Maríano wouldn't tell me. There was only so much he could do."

"I wish I knew."

"Don't be pompous," Chaim said sharply. "You've had far too much to drink." A breeze swept over the sea: Chaim felt a pleasant draft under his armpits. "It's all very simple. Take this envelope and on Thursday I'll be in the Gare du Nord to meet you. A honeymoon in Paris! What more could you want?"

André refilled his glass. "I can't take the money. Don't be silly."

Chaim pushed the envelope towards him. He was glad about the wind. In the evening he felt younger and almost slim. "Look, they are probably raiding the club right now," he said. "If they find me I'm screwed. Take the money if only for Toni's sake. How could you ever get out? I'll have a new passport by nine o'clock. Tomorrow morning I'll be in Tangier. Wednesday afternoon I'll be in Paris. It's all very simple. Take it."

"I don't understand. Why did you have a forged passport? I thought you were an American citizen."

Chaim sighed. It seemed so long ago. The silly women on the boat, Le Havre, Isaac thin and worried. Becky, Becky. It has been so long since you left me. So much has happened.

"I was broke. I sold my American passport in '47."

"You sold it!"

"There is no need to go into that now. Take the money."

André, slightly drunk, stared out at the sea. Bombs had made a ruin of the port years ago. The guts of several maimed sheds raised themselves like ghosts into the cool and darkening sky. About fifty feet out to sea a garden of barnacles climbed out of the oily water and held the hull of a sunken tanker in a death-grip. The rotting hull, wallowing in filth and mud, was bloated and like a corpse. The slogan SIEMPRE FRANCO was painted on it. André lit a cigarette off his butt. "It's wrong, you know. They have no right. Stay here and we'll fight it."

"Child, fight what? They say I was a smuggler. That's true. They say I'm here on a false passport. That's true. You've had too much cognac. Also, I'm sorry to say, you are very young. There are the times to fight and the times to run. Knowing that is the difference between being a foolish hero or a useful man. Take the money!"

André swallowed his cognac belligerently, but he stuffed the envelope in his pocket.

Chaim called for the bill. "I'm going to miss the flamenco," he said. "Tell Toni I'm sorry I didn't see her. Have a nice wedding, *Mazel Tov*. Thursday night I'll take you to the Café de Paris for dinner."

"Was it Kraus?"

"Always it has to be your fault. Maybe you're only an intellectual after all. How could he have known about my passport?"

"He worked for you. He might have heard gossip."

"It wasn't Kraus," Chaim said. "But you keep out of his way."

"Why?"

"He doesn't like you. He likes Toni."

"I'm not exactly nuts about him myself."

"Don't be a tough guy."

Chaim paid the bill. "Well, so I've been to Spain," he said.

"And what did you find?"

"Find?"

"Yes."

"You are very young."

"You keep saying that."

"Don't be angry. It's just that *my* hair is falling out."

The sky was softening, André noticed. It was the colour of melancholy. The cognac felt warm in his belly, his arms dropped languorously beside him . . . if it would stop now, *right now.* . . .

"Why are you helping me, Chaim? Got my salvation all figured out?"

"Don't be a silly boy."

André grinned nastily.

"I have faith in men," Chaim said. "I would rather act on that faith than be miserable and without it like you."

"But maybe I'm right just the same, eh, Chaim?"

"Maybe, but is that really important?" Chaim got up. "It's stupid to talk," he said. "Paint this; the sea, the sky, evening, two men talking, one angry, the other old."

"What if I loved her and I was mad?"

"Now where in the hell did you get that idea?"

"My grandfather was mad. In his last years anyway. They say I get it from him."

"You're not mad, André. A bit crazy perhaps."

They shook hands. André felt small and poor in spirit.

"André . . ." Chaim began shyly. He shuffled from one foot to another. It was the first time André had ever seen him embarrassed. It made him, André, feel insecure. Chaim was, had to be, unshakable. "In case . . ." He began again. "No, that's silly. Look, *boychick*, you're a fine painter. Paint always. I believe in you."

André smiled self-consciously. "I'm going, Chaim. This kind of farewell stuff upsets me. Good luck, old man."

"I'll see you on Thursday."

"Well, I hope so, anyway."

Chaim watched him walk away. I will never see him again, he thought. "Cosmi," he called. "Cosmi, bring me another bottle of muscatel."

VI

Chaim was gone.

André sat in a bar on the Calle de Sangre and he ordered another drink. He felt trapped and alone and the cognac was not doing him any good yet. His head was full of pain and he could not think clearly. One more drink, just one, he thought, and then I'll go up to Toni's.

The next bar was practically empty and he left after one drink.

Finally he found a bar that suited him. It was dilapidated, anonymous, and there were many flies. Labourers, leathery-faced, sat around woodenly. The oily waiter, who waddled and had no neck, was probably a German. André called him over.

He was a Belgian. *Oui*, he had been in the Legion and fought in many *guerres*. *Afrique du Nord*, Spaneesh land (*oui*, he spoke Eng-lissh), against *les nègres* when there were *grèves*, and against *les boches*, *claro*, in the Great War. André told him to go away. And to himself he thought, feeling fine on the cognac now, how do you say f—— off in Spanish. He must ask Pepe.

Pepe. He was invited there for dinner. . . .

André spilled his drink on the table and with his finger he traced wet designs on the wood. He did a drawing of the waiter. He was lying on a tray, surrounded by vegetables, and there was an apple in his mouth.

André got up.

It was still twilight. He thought: This is the interval, all the world is sighing human, time for vermouth and mild applejack, whisky blanc for the habitants in St. Jovite and a lucky other few, rest for the unknowing men, unfocus.

> *Dere's no hidin' place down dere,*
> *Dere's no hidin' place down dere,*
> *Oh I went to de rock to hide my face,*
> *De rock cried out, "No hidin' place,"*
> *Dere's no hidin' place down dere.*

Whoops, don't totter.

The street, hazy, was cradled by a warming light. On a street bench an aged gypsy woman held a newspaper cupped under her chin. She smiled into the cooling sky, a saucerful of sun quivering in her frail grip. Her hands were livid, death was coming. But squinting into the going-away sun she seemed happy at last to be unaware of people warped by greed and misery passing quickly.

André kneeled down by the bench and kissed the gypsy woman's hand. He looked up at her, and he said: "Sing me a song."

He let his head fall on her lap.

She laughed. Her teeth, there were only three, were yellow. "I'm too old," she said.

"Then I'll sing for you. But, mind you, it's in American." He began:

> *Oh de rock cried out, "I'm burnin' too,"*
> *Oh de rock cried out, "I'm burnin' too,"*
> *Oh de rock cried out, "I'm burnin' too,"*
> *I want to go to hebb'n as well as you,*
> *Dere's no hidin' place down dere.*

The old woman applauded. André kissed her again, and skipped away.

In the next bar André made a speech in French. The men applauded, wineskins were passed around, and altogether they sang *Los Quatro Generales*. Afterwards André stood up on a table and recited, or tried to recite, *I Sing of Olaf* in Spanish. He told them the poem had been written by a great man in a stifled land where, nevertheless, there were many great men. He told them stories about the great men and he tried to teach them how to sing *Alouette*. Then, he confided in them. He said: "I am a mad man."

He left the bar, and the men made him promise to come back. The bartender said: "*Como su casa.*"

Outside, André sang:

> *Oh de sinner man he gambled an' fell,*
> *Oh de sinner man he gambled an' fell,*
> *Oh de sinner man gambled, he gambled an' fell;*
> *He wanted to go to hebben, but he had to go to hell,*
> *Dere's no hidin' place down dere.*

He stepped into the doorway of her rooming house and suddenly a chill came over him. He began to climb the stairs and on the second landing he met Kraus. André, tottering, stopped and stared. Kraus, oddly enough, appeared frightened. André laughed.

"I'm charmed to . . ."

"Oh, not again. What are you doing here?"

"Are you going up to her room in your drunken condition?" Kraus asked.

André shoved his hands in his pockets. He hoped that Kraus would not notice that he was shivering. "What do you want from us?" he asked.

A twitch developed on Kraus's lip and André felt triumphant.

"Well . . . ?"

Kraus's face seemed ashen in the poor light of the hallway.

"I do not want to fight you," Kraus said.

"What?"

"She, Theresa . . ."

"What about Chaim?"

Kraus shrugged his shoulders.

"So it was you!"

"Yes."

Yes, just like that. Yes.

André laughed. He laughed and laughed and laughed. He laughed because Chaim was a useful man and he laughed because Kraus was a brute. He clutched the banister and doubled up laughing. He laughed because Ida was dead and he laughed because probably he did not love Toni. He laughed because he was drunk. He laughed and laughed. He laughed because he was feverish and he laughed because the doctors said he would go mad. Tears rolled down his cheeks, and he laughed.

Kraus slapped him and André stopped laughing. "You are mad," he said.

"She wouldn't let you touch her."

And for an instant, briefly, they stared into each other's eyes.

"I am going to kill you," André said, and he continued up the stairs again, trying not to stagger.

His head was throbbing and he was soaked in sweat. He knew the symptoms of his migraines backwards, but he pretended not to know. He opened up the door to the room. Toni was dressing.

She jumped up when she saw him. "André!"

"I just met Kraus on the stairs."

"André, you look ill. Did he hit you?"

"I'm not ill. I'm drunk."

"Oh."

Golden legs climbing into a skirt.

André handed her a cigarette. He lit it for her. "Did you get into bed with him?"

"Yes."

"Did he force you?"

"No."

All he could see was the two of them in bed. She, in his arms, panting.

"You must try to understand André. He was crying like a child. I felt sorry for him."

Still, something was broken. He felt empty. "I understand," he lied. "I love you and I understand."

She came into his arms and he shivered.

"André, you're ill. Your skin is burning."

He sat down uneasily. His eyes were not so much shocked as absolutely innocent and uncomprehending. "Chaim is leaving Spain tonight," he said. "They closed the club, he was here on a false passport. Roger told them, probably because of us."

"Oh, André."

Yeah, he thought. I know. Oh, André. "We will get married tomorrow, and join him in Paris on Thursday."

Toni puffed deeply on her cigarette and a hollow formed in her cheeks. Her hair was all tangled up. She turned on him suddenly, her eyes passionately deep. "Do you really want to marry me?"

"I don't know."

"André, don't be angry. It would mean leaving my country, my people. You never really loved me. You feel sorry for me. That is not enough."

"Does he love you?"

"You don't understand. I love you, André, but I don't know if it would work out."

He sat down beside her on the bed and for a long time he stroked her hair gently.

Finally, she said, "What shall we do?"

"Come to France with me."

"All right."

He got up. "I'll see you in the morning," he said.

"Where are you going?"

"To my room. I don't feel well. I think I'll paint for a while."

"No drinking?"

"I don't really mind that you went to bed with him," he said.

"Do you want me to come with you now?"

"No. Not now."

He walked over to her again and stroked her black hair. "You are beautiful," he said.

She smiled.

"Is it, Toni . . . Do you think that I cannot love?"

"There is something rotten inside you. Together we shall fight it."

"Good-bye."

"*Hasta mañana.*"

"*Si, guapa.*"

VII

What was that song?

> *Yes, I'm leavin', leavin', Mama,*
> *Oo' – But I don't know whichaway to go.*
> *I'm leavin', leavin', Mama,*
> *But I don't know which way to go.*

He was slipping down a ladder, every rung rejecting him.
The bottle was on the floor beside the bed.
Another drink.
André could not sleep.
The bed was a ship whirling in a stormy sea yet standing still at the same time.

His body was no longer a well-integrated unit but instead a bunch of ridiculous, unrelated items. Something to be tabulated, like clothing returned from the laundry. Some arms, some legs, a few organs and private parts, so many fingers and dirty feet, and a head twirling, superfluous and independent, in still faraway water. He would have lifted up his arm to anchor his floating head but he knew if he did this his arm would snap off. Also that his fingers were molasses and if he attempted to grasp the bedpost they would stick to the metal in puddles. *God will punish you*, his father always used to say. The grating hullabaloo of the rats fussing in the woodwork came to him again and he slipped down further under the blankets to keep his head from being exposed. An hour's sweat had dried on his body. The itch was a constant agony. *He was going mad!* He laughed weakly.

Sentences, not thoughts, came –

A body and a head, thin body big head, are lying on my bed.

I am a madman,
this is my spout.

Pour me out,
pour me out.

In the neighbourhood theatre somebody or something like him was doing fiendish things on the screen; sometimes the yahoo on the screen and his more rational self would snap into an idiot focus, but the fusion was always blurred.

I'm dead! Tomorrow I'm going to come back and look at my dead body and tickle my dead body, tomorrow after breakfast. I wonder if my dead body will look peaceful like dead bodies are supposed to look? *Yo-yo-hum and a bottle of rum.* The corpse will have to be shipped back to America for mama and that's going to cost money. *Cash, brother, cash. Put up or shut up!*

Slowly the madness in him subsided. *Entr'acte* for the damned. Time for drinks and time for cakes. Exhausted, breathing heavily, he lay back on his pillow sinking abysmally. . . .

The elastic mustn't snap. . . .

What if the whole bed is full of them, he thought. What if right now a rat is picking at the dandruff in my hair? Suddenly he trembled. *Now I'm travelling through that undiscovered country from whose bourn* . . . He pleaded with the engulfing vagueness. I'm up! Jesus, I even know what's going on. He tested this last thought aloud to find out about his voice. The sounds were jarring but he recognised it as his own flat untuneful baritone. Winding through a spinning progression of questions and answers he soon convinced himself that everything stinging in the bed was him. *The Lord giveth and the Lord taketh away.* The rats are scribbling prophecies on the ceiling and jitterbugging on my floor. Madman boogie! He tried to laugh. (Turn over the record, jack.) The upshot was a lunatic cackle in an empty subway. Next he tried to bribe himself about switching on the lights. If he did this there would at least be a cigarette. Unable to hoist himself into any conclusion he began to whine and think about home, about why he had ever left and if he could ever possibly go back. . . .

It was the London nightmare again.

A real empty stomach and a rotting soul, flaking at the sides, walked love and love through the purple bomb-gutted streets of the victorious city. The yellow pasteboard moon hanging like a bright lollypop in the black sky illuminated a building on Old Kent Road. From the other side the building was really only a wall. While waiting for the fall of the man who had entered a window on the fourth storey of the building that was only a wall, a stinging hose of urine ran down André's right trouser leg. The man must have never quite fallen to the bottom as he stood there and stood there for three whole weeks without ever hearing a goddam sound. The fetor of his own dry urine mixed with the floating ambrosial stink of the dead violet flowers being pumped on to the pavement through the drainpipes. Ernie, hollow-eyed spiv with a No face, sold American-made nylons on Trafalgar Square.

A perfume advert, posted in neon dream blood over the Haymarket.

Out of the heavens – to you!
MY SIN
de inez blumberg

Ernie ruined at least three pairs when a sore burst under his thumbnail and running green pus cascaded over the silk in a blinding viscous fountain. From the top of his colonnade a one-eyed admiral of another time and place tottered precariously as the pigeons heaped still more piles of excrement on the gawking tourists below. The young bobby with a foreign gaffer in his arms beamed while a stray arm snapped the shutter of a Kodak, exploding the whole area in a firecracker of light. Simultaneously and nearby a Welsh whore spat. Nobody noticed. Rats floating by in pools of gangrene had clogged the streets again.

One thing I'll say about the Limeys, a man waving a copy of *Time* magazine shouted, they sure can take it!

On insecure concrete bases the imperial lions drooped lugubriously, nicotinic teeth beginning to crack and fall. Hairless bodies, pimpled bodies, gleaming like rotting meat in the sun. Nobody had been kind enough to tear out their eyes so André rushed over and wrenched them out with the branch of a dead tree. A professionally blind pauper woman approached an enlightened whore with flowers. TWO BOB! I wouldn't wipe me bloody arse with your flowers.

I wonder, another tourist with an airmail copy of *Superman* comics folded under his arm wondered, whether we'll ever be able to make anything of this?

Flung into Westminster Abbey on the tide of a frantic mob André saw more Kodaks and women chewing gum trample on the tombs of Samuel Butler and Charles Dickens. He got the idea and began to pick vigorously at his ass while standing on Alex Pope. The guide obliged his fact-greedy audience, informing them that as the abbey was so jammed with the immortal dead many of the poets were buried standing up. If there's no more room, André considered aloud, burn my body on hot flame and sprinkle my ashes in the public urinals. When the Russians arrive they may piss their guts out on my cranium. Vomit got stuck in his throat and to avoid suffocation he rushed outside. *Ida loves Manny '48* was carved on the railing of Westminster Bridge.

For several ages he stumble-wandered through the twilight alleys of Soho drinking and vomiting up blood-red wines like a *consommé* of an anger offered up as a hate-broth to the gods.

Later, in Piccadilly, he got angry with Eros. With a handy can-opener he ripped open his stomach, wrapping a mile of slimy intestines around a railing while rent flesh flapped in the wind. Tossing leaking kidneys heavenwards he studied his heart, mouldy but still beating, on the pavement. A legless orphan with a bent arm and his nose on sideways gave him a quick shove before he could finish disembowelling himself. The spectre snarled; move on, gov'ner, we've seen all this before.

He took to flight, racing across oceans and worlds, but he could not escape the mockery of the whores chuckling in the vacuum.

Eighteen tiny red dots behind six others of an unusual shade of green floated to and fro in the mist. So after all, André aroused to semi-consciousness penetrated the fog, so after all . . .

If he switched on the lights he would have to see the rats! His cigarettes were nearby on the table and he managed to light one in the dark. Listening to the darkness, he was conscious of the sharp scuffle of the rats and the loud beating of his heart. Puffing flaccidly at his cigarette, his last link with sanity, he tried to shake from his mind the persistent visual image of a decapitated dead rat. Inky spurts of blood trickled slowly out of the rat's neck. The grey body coughed convulsively and the belly gradually flattened out like a punctured tube. He watched the lighted end of his cigarette butt shudder in the darkness. There was no longer an outer objective world. (And perhaps, he thought with sudden delirious vision, there never was.)

Finally, and with many misgivings, he switched on the light. A rat scurried across the bedroom floor and slithered in under the cupboard door. Another, more formidable rat looked up slyly and amazed from atop the heap of soiled laundry piled under the sink. They stared at each other for an instant – the rat whisking his long tail closer around him and the man shaking.

The rat darted across the room and slid in under the bed.

His cigarette dropped to the floor. He was completely undone. Useless, not dead and not alive but hovering fitfully, he pushed his head down deep into the bedding and bit hard into the pillow. And he lay there, sliding about in his own sweat, for a good half hour.

Bottle on the floor.

Another drink, huh?

> *Oo – an' I feel like lyin' down.*
> *An' I feel like walking, mama,*
> *I feel like walkin', mama,*
> *An' I feel like lyin' down.*

VIII

Valencia, April 19, 1951

"What can she see in him? He is a drunkard and probably mad. It is certainly that she is young and romantic.

"What a glorious afternoon! What a personal triumph! It is true that at first she was reticent, that she professed foolish loyalties to the boy, but once I had mastered her how eager she was for more! I shall not immediately talk of marriage. It would be bad for her. Theresa will be difficult at first, but Antonita's modest ways will soon win her. It shall be Theresa's duty to train the child in the ways of society. For I know now that soon I shall be needed again. Hermann writes from Rome that he has been appointed to an important post in Argentina. Paul is doing his background credit in the Belgian Congo. The Afrika Korps meets regularly now. Perhaps I shall be called next? As soon as I am repatriated I can count on a high position in the new army. An American Ambassador in Madrid is a healthy sign. Perhaps I should write to him? Theresa could do the letter for me. How it will please her to see us reorganised, returning to our old work with a new vigour! She will stop moping about her Alfred (for she does, even if she refuses to admit it), and my wife will be able to help her. I . . ."

"Writing again?" Theresa asked, after she had entered the room quietly.

Roger smiled good-naturedly. "My journal," he said.

"You are in good spirits lately," she said.

"Theresa . . ." Roger began slowly, "if – well, if his kind had won the mobs would be – there would be no order. Isn't that true?"

"How many times have I told you not to speak of him?"

"I would kill him for you!"

Theresa laughed. "It is too late, Roger dear. He is dead."

Dead, yes. Then why is he always in the room? He thought of saying so, at least asking (for she knew everything), but then he thought better of it. "You think of him too much," he said meekly.

"I regret ever having known him," she said, enunciating each word clearly. "Now, are you pleased?"

Roger laughed and shut his diary. "Theresa, do you like me? Do you enjoy having me near you?"

"Like you? Why I adore you! I couldn't live without you."

"Don't joke."

Laughing, Theresa tossed her head back. He watched the Adam's apple bobbing on her neck. She stopped laughing as quickly as she had begun. "What does it matter?" she asked.

"Don't laugh at me!"

"Why not? What does it matter?"

Roger looked down at his boots and he rolled up his fists so that his fingernails dug into the palms of his hands. "I had news from Hermann this morning," he said. "He is going to Argentina. Everywhere calls are coming. It will be our turn soon. Won't that delight you?"

"Our turn? What need have they of an idiot colonel and his old maid sister? Will they put you in charge of the inspection of brothels?"

Her joke seemed to delight her. She giggled, held her hand to her mouth, and giggled again.

"Have you been drinking?"

"Drinking? Roger, you surprise me!"

Roger shrugged his shoulders and laughed playfully. He made a funny face at her.

"Stop it!" she shrieked menacingly.

"But I don't mind if you have been drinking."

"I have not been drinking!"

Roger looked down at his boots again.

"What would you do without me, Roger?"

"Without you?"

"What if something should happen to me? Or if I should run away with a man?"

"Oh, you are only joking. You wouldn't run away with a man!"

She lurched, falling into the armchair by the table. "Do you mean that a man wouldn't run away with me?"

"No, Theresa. No, not at all."

Now, for the first time, he noticed that she was wearing lipstick. Her hair had been done in a new style and she was wearing high heels. He smiled and she realised that he was amused.

"Where were you all afternoon?" she asked coldly.

"Walking."

"Where, walking?"

"Just walking."

"You still lie like a little boy. Here you talk of ideals and position but all you can really think of is your ugly sexual lusts. Is that the way Hermann got his position?"

"You talk nonsense!"

"They make baby-talk, they joke about you, then they drink and make love again. What do you expect? He is so much younger than you are. Oh, it's a wonderful joke!"

Roger's lip began to twitch.

"She is a whore, Roger."

"I don't know what you are talking about!"

"Fine, colonel. You don't know. But I should watch out for the Jew. He is shrewd and not unintelligent. But then I forgot, you have so much in common. Both of you are whoremasters!"

"I will not stand for this!"

Theresa laughed, holding her hands to her mouth. "I should watch out for gonorrhoea, my boy. I doubt if she is very particular about her bed companions."

"I am going out."

She got up and shouted into his ear. "Do you know what he did? He sent up one of his comrades, a bartender, to spy on us. He made improper advances. I had to throw him out. But you are afraid of the boy. You are afraid!"

"I do not want to fight the artist!"

"He sent up a spy. To me, your sister!"

He was sweating. "I don't want to kill. Not any more."

She held him in her thin arms and shook him. "*They hate us.* Show them a weakness, just once, and you are done for. They will organise. He, the Jew, and the others. Let them know, let them even suspect, and we are done for. You must kill him, Roger. You have no choice!"

"I'm going out. I . . ."

He raced down the stairs.

"Go! Run to her! Satyr!"

As soon as the door had been banged shut she picked up his diary.

IX

"Derek?"

It was still not midnight. Derek, two pillows propped under his head, lolled carelessly on the bed. On the night table beside him was a bottle of gin and a half-filled glass. The window was open and the curtains fluttered. His shoes were off, he was barechested. He was twirling the hairs on his chest and wiggling his toes. His eyes were blood-shot and not focusing properly. "I am ruminating," he said.

Barney hesitated in the doorway. Not in all the years that he had known him had he ever been alone with Derek. But now the idea of sipping gin in a hotel room with another man, even if that other man was Derek, appealed to him. "May I come in?" he asked.

Derek indicated the armchair by the window with a sweeping gesture of his left leg. "*Avante,*" he said.

Barney collapsed in the armchair. He pulled out his handkerchief and mopped the sweat off his forehead. "I can't find Jessie," he said. "I'm worried. I don't know what's happened to her."

"Jessica. Faithless Jessica. Perhaps she has eloped with a Bengalese banana planter? No, that's not it. She's gone into a nunnery. Elected silence and all that. Cut off your left ear and send it to her in a box."

"Don't be so funny!"

"Pour yourself a drink, *compañero.*"

Barney got up and poured himself a gin. He found the icewater on the floor beside the bed.

"So Lazarus drinks with the *Goyim,*" Derek said.

"Why not?" Barney sat down again. "And I don't mind you calling me Lazarus."

Derek refilled his glass. "What's wrong, Barney?"

"Do you know where she is?"

"No."

"I found her kissing André in the room last night. We quarrelled, and she tossed me out. I . . . Well, I didn't come home until morning. She wasn't in the room."

"You think she spent the night with André?"

"After I left the club last night two hundred bucks were missing from my wallet. Either Jessie took it and gave it to

André, or he took it himself." Barney pulled out his handkerchief and mopped his forehead again. "It's not the money, but . . ."

"Why don't you leave her?"

Barney trembled. "How can I leave her?" he asked.

"What do you mean, how?"

"We've got two kids."

Derek gulped down his drink and poured himself another glass. Barney got up and looked out of the window. "Those falyas are kind of pretty. Too bad they're gonna burn them."

"Maybe they have to burn them?"

"Why?"

"Perhaps in all of us there is some evil and we're just too weak to burn it. So we build evil toys and dance around them, later we burn them. Hoping, perhaps, that it will help."

"You think they have to burn them then?"

"It all depends on who's watching."

"I don't understand."

Derek tittered. "Okay then, let's talk about me."

Barney turned towards Derek, his eyes were startled and afraid. "What's wrong with you?" he asked.

Derek sat up in bed and bowed from the waist. "I am a homosexual," he said.

Barney blushed. "Yeah, well, I mean we all know."

"Yes, we all know! But nobody talks about it. Okay, so let's both sit on the floor and talk about me being a homo."

"What's there to talk about?"

Derek snickered. "Barney, you are *formidable!* Sometimes I wish Jessie and myself just hadn't happened to you."

"You could see a doctor, I guess."

Derek giggled. He caught a peek of himself in the mirror and he shook his head so that his hair would get all mussed up. "*Olé!* Sit down, amigo. I regret that I have only one bottle to give up for America. Pour yourself another drink."

Barney sat down again and his shoulders sagged. He took a sip of his drink. "Why do you always treat me as if I was a jerk? You guys who went to Spain and all that were supposed to be interested in your fellow men. Well, waddiya think I am?"

Derek smiled solemnly. "I am no longer the man who went to Spain. The years since then have separated the men from the boys. *Et voilà*, one of the boys!"

Barney lit a cigar. "I know what you people think. I'm vulgar, I haven't had an education, I never read any books. Everything I've done I had to do for myself. I would have liked to be cultured and to be able to say nice things in company, like you or Jessie. But I had to grow up quick. Okay, so it'll be different for my kids. They'll go to college and be doctors or something. Not only that but I'm going to get them both life subscriptions to the Book-of-the-Month Club and the *Atlantic Monthly*. I know that literature does good things for a person. It gives him class. When I get home I'm going to get the kids a gramophone and a few hundred bucks' worth of classical music. We Jews are a musical people you know.

"I come from an orthodox family. Not that religion does a guy any harm, but my old man was sort of old-fashioned for America. I mean when I married Jessie he went into mourning for me just as if I was dead. He died a little later and he wrote in his will that I shouldn't come to his funeral. My mother is helpless with rheumatism. Three times I offered to send her to the springs or Florida but my money isn't kosher. She won't even see my children to bless them – her own flesh and blood. So you see Jessie cost me a lot and I want to keep her."

Barney took another sip of gin, mopped his forehead again, and laughed helplessly.

"You know that song," he said. "I think it goes *It's Only a Barnum and Bailey World, Just as Phony as Can Be*. I'm not good at tunes. But that's the way I feel about things. That's the way life's been kind of. Barnum and Bailey. Phony.

"When you're fifteen, well you figure that when you're twenty-one everything is going to be fun and games, but then it isn't so. So you figure that maybe when you're thirty you'll be able to relax, but you just go on and on.

"You get real worked up about a movie star. She looks like a million bucks on the screen. So you see her in real life and she's just another whore. Or when you're working damn hard on the road you think one day I'm going to get married and everything will be fun and games and love, like in that picture *Claudia* with Dorothy McGuire. So you get married and you find out. Or you really admire some couple you know, make them out for heroes, they're always so happy and crazy about each other. So you pick up the paper one morning and you find out they got a divorce. And then the bright guys, I mean the kids who always got good marks and stayed home to read books, well you figure that at least they made out good. So you walk into a bar one day and they're drunk and trying to stick you for a fiver. And the guys I used to know who became commies. Well they either turned out to be queers or they married a rich girl and became clothing manufacturers like everybody else.

"Like the really smart-looking girls you used to know and now you meet them on the street and they're fat and trying to get you to make them even if they've got husbands. Well I was brought up to believe that you married a woman and she was yours and she loved you, like my parents, but I found out different. Why do guys always fool around with each other's wives? I respect other people's property. Why can't we all work and mind our own business? I mean if a guy's not lazy and he's got a bit of brains he can still make his way. I don't ask no favours. Why can't everybody be like that? Do you see what I mean? I mean I know that there are some things you can't buy with money, like friendship or health. But I don't see why if I worked so hard all my life so that I could have it easy when I was old I should give my money to guys who were just too lazy to sweat like me. Do you think communism is fair? It's sort of robbery in a way. I'm not unkind, I support charities. But what I worked so hard for should be for me and my children."

Derek began to pick furiously at a particular hair on his chest. Suddenly he yanked it out. "It was grey," he said.

Barney poured himself another drink.

"Barney, leave her. She's rotten. She hates you."

"Hates me?" A shudder ran through him. "Did she ever tell you that?"

"No."

Barney grinned. Suddenly he turned to Derek. "Why do you drink so much?" he asked.

Derek sat up in bed. "Why don't you divorce Jessie?"

"But what's the real reason? I mean before Spain you were never like that. You were always writing or going to meetings. Maybe Europe isn't good for you?"

"It had nothing to do with Europe or Spain. It all happened inside me, *compañero*. Slowly. It wasn't dramatic so I fabricated the drama. I hated America so I joined picket lines, I loved Spain so I fought in a war. But I didn't truly love Spain or hate America, I *decided* to feel these things. I keep telling myself that some day I'm going to snap out of it and produce something. A play, one poem, a thought, an act, anything! Meanwhile I keep on drinking and hating myself and waiting for death. The truth is I'm bored. I can enjoy nothing. Barney, I'm an impotent man!"

Barney began to fidget in his chair. He did not know what to say. So he smiled lamely, and he said: "I guess we all have our troubles."

Derek poured himself another drink. "If I decided to go back to the States would you give me a job?" he asked.

"Yes. Certainly."

"No. It wouldn't work."

"Why? We could be friends."

"As a matter of fact we couldn't."

Barney got up and stared out of the window. There was a faint ringing in his ears and he felt dizzy. He put down his drink. "You know I was in a whorehouse last night," he said.

"Sweeney among the Nightingales."

"What?"

"I was just being supercilious. Pay no attention."

Barney began to sweat again. "Look, I'll be frank. You have a lot of influence over Jessie, right?"

"Perhaps."

"You come home with us and stick close to her. Live with us. See that she doesn't screw around. Tell her that she's got kids. Well, you know what I mean. I'll give you a good allowance. You won't have to work or anything."

"It wouldn't work."

"Why wouldn't it work?"

"You can't do these things with money."

Barney laughed cynically. "You may have been around but so have I. You'd be surprised what you can do with money. For five hundred bucks I could get that André kid to lock her out of his room."

"What makes you think she's fooling around with him?"

"Come home. I'll give you two hundred bucks a week."

"Don't be silly!"

"I know how you get your money. Jessie sends it to you. I could have you cut off."

"I guess I've been underestimating you."

"I won't have our marriage broken up."

"Would people laugh at you?"

"That's no way to talk."

"Get out, Barney."

"What?"

"I'm expecting a boy-friend."

"You're just a goddam queer. I should have known better."

Derek got out of bed and opened up the door. "That's no way to start off a business relationship," he said.

"I'm sorry. It's . . . well, I lost my temper. Come on, let's shake on it."

"So long, Barney."

"You mean you're not coming?"

"No. And just in passing. It was me, I stole your two hundred bucks."

"Do you know where Jessie is?"

"No."

"Well you tell her when I find her I'm going to break her neck."

Derek laughed, and Barney slammed the door.

x

Pepe rushed into the room, and he was laughing. "Where is my wife?" he yelled. "Who has run off with her? My wife who is going to have a boy, where is she?"

María was sitting up in bed. Several pillows were propped up behind her. She was wearing the lovely shawl that had belonged to her grandmother. She smiled.

"Ah, there she is! Well tell her that her husband has inherited a fortune!" He tossed a bundle of bills on the blanket. "Seventy-five pesetas. Count it!"

"Pepe! Where did you get it?"

Pepe howled and slapped his thighs. "It is my army pension. The very excellent Generalissimo Franco, Chief of our State, has decided to issue pensions to veterans of the Fifth Regiment."

"Where did you get the money?"

Pepe sat down on the bed. He kissed María, and pulled her hair.

"Pepe!"

"Look!" he said. He produced a bouquet of flowers from behind his back. "For my wife who is going to have triplets."

"I know! André has sold another picture."

"No."

"Chaim?"

"No."

"Where did you get the money?"

"Last night our friend Luís who is an anarchist picked up an American tourist and showed him all the wonderful sights of our city. The kind American rewarded him handsomely." He dug into his jacket pocket and pulled out a bottle of manzanilla. "Where is André? I thought he was coming for supper."

"He must have forgotten."

Pepe noticed that the table was set for a feast. All the cutlery had been polished, the linen napkins were out, there was a bottle of wine and three loaves of bread. "How could he have forgotten? Did you see him today?"

"No."

María shrugged her shoulders. "All that food," she said. Pepe kissed her solemnly. "Are you in pain?" he asked.

"No."

"It will be a boy."

"Why do you keep saying that? What if it is a girl?"

"It will be a boy." Pepe noticed the table again and he felt badly. "It isn't like him. He seldom forgets."

"Perhaps he is ill again?"

Pepe rolled himself a cigarette. He had planned on a truly wonderful evening with his wife and his best friend. "Why should he be ill?" he asked.

"There are many reasons. He is unhappy, and he has no church."

"Must you always bring religion into it?"

"Are you upset about something?"

"No."

She coughed. The pain came again, quickly.

"In a way you are right," he said. "He is unhappy. But I am glad that they can't get the educated people or the artists. It makes me feel good that he does not believe in God."

"I pray for him every morning. I have been doing it for months."

Pepe groaned impatiently. "He doesn't need your prayers!" he said.

"He has killed. It is a sin."

"Only when the church kills it isn't a sin."

"The church never kills. It is only the priests."

"Look, he doesn't believe in it. None of us do!" There was a note of desperation in his voice. "How many times must I tell you that?"

"He may not think he does but I know differently."

"Sure. You know all about it."

"God believes in him."

Pepe laughed. "You will drive me mad," he said. "It is a bad thing that he has killed. It will ruin him."

"I told you a hundred times that it wasn't his fault."

"If it had been his fault it wouldn't have mattered so much. Don't you understand?"

"You know," he said. "You know everything."

XI

On the calle de Sangre, André in a delirium stumbles onwards for six blocks before he is able to assess his surroundings with any degree of penetration. Mechanically he looks at his wristwatch: it is 12:30 a.m. This, he acknowledges, is a fact, recognition of which is a condition of sanity.

Darkness, buildings looming, rot eating into walls. Lamp posts like the luminous yellow spittle of gnarled immobile cripples. Neon café lights, wavering kaleidoscopic breeze in a cash-and-carry limbo, advertising particular brands of glitter death. Mock halos rounding yellow lamps.

He pauses at the Plaza del Mercado, then turns leftwards towards the sea. Cold in his lungs, suspended, seeps into his bones. His feet are wet lumps of bread floating on icy water, his head a soggy sponge. I live inside a polluted womb, he thinks, and dismissing this thought he tries to think of something funny. Chaim in the army, Toni a nun, his mother in a chorus line. *Ho-ho!* He remembers Paris . . .

When he had first arrived it had been summer. He had got off the metro at Saint Germain-des-Prés and a stale sun hung like a drying lemon in the sky. (He remembered thinking just that when he had climbed the metro steps on to the street.) Men with beards, and women sloppily dressed, idled obligingly at the sidewalk café tables, just as they always did for picture stories in *Life* or *Collier's*.

Paris is skeletons copulating on tin roofs and the culminating corpse of a dead civilisation dying and raising a stench to jeering heaven while toasting on the wicked flames of wanton ennui and sin. Intellectual maggots crawling, sucking, impervious to their own horrid secretions. (No grand bang finale here.) The aimless, the destitute, the degenerate. Integrity cheap at five cents a cup, souls going quick at bargain basement prices, love liberated on tap in cafés and dim doorways. Clearing-house international for queers with pinch-polly asses and googoo eyes. (God, they say in the Reine Blanche, is a Queen.) Aged discards fishing for their souls in the Seine and not getting even a nibble. Boring depravity shimmying like hep sin in the Tabou. (God is a hipster and when he wakes of from dis l'il ole dream dat is us he's gonna have himself a real ball.) Jitterbug becomes philosophy and boogie-woogie love. (Do you believe in God? The old man in the *jardins* giggled. Wouldn't you, he said?)

I shall grow old and die not knowing.

Buildings, like bloated lungs gasping, and a café open. A gang of ragged soldiers, a drunken boy, a few labourers and two floozies, are drinking *vino blanco* and singing:

> *Ay! puerto moro de Tanger*
> *puerto que me vio marchar*
> *en un barquito de espuma*
> *por la esmeralda del mar.*

Unmelodious wail flowing, deranged plaint of dead souls. Tumbling, rolling, screaming. People in a circle around a soldier, homemade guitar, woeful voice. Together, clapping, singing, taking turns at verses, dumb despair tumbling on endlessly, spiritual hemophilia.

> *Yo soy pobre emigrante*
> *que traigo a esta tierra extraña*
> *en mi pecho uno estandarte*
> *con los colores de España.*

Drunken boy clambers up on the bar, sigh of wonder up from the crowd, he kicks his feet down sharply, music leaping, a floozie tosses off her jacket and jumps up to join him. Crowd yelling, crowd clapping. Girl flings her body about, legs kicking, tears rolling down her cheeks. Sweaty boy stamping, bending backwards again, dancing around her. . . .

> *Por mi patria y por mi novia*
> *y mi Virgen de San Gil*
> *y mi rosario de cuentas*
> *yo me quisiera morir.*

André felt exposed, dazzled as well, as if suddenly a secret door to his soul had swung ajar. There was something hauntingly abysmal about their song. Perhaps, he thought, if the unknown can never become known it can at least be sung. *(God, simply, is what we do not know.)* He felt as if he was living within a memory, that this experience must be only so that it might become a part of his spiritual past. Then the door swung shut.

But the abysmal something was still there.

> *Mundos y planetas en "revolución"*
> *con el fuego! fuego! de mi "corazón"!*

The girl, he did not know her, took him by the arm and dragged him into the bar. The makeup on her face had streaked. Her cheeks were hollow and her eyes were dark. She had a woman's body, she tried to walk like a woman, but her mannerisms were those of a deficient child.

"Who are you?"

"My name is Lolita."

"Lolita?"

Perhaps, somewhere, he had known a Lolita? But he had known so many things.

"I come from Cadiz. My mother was a kitchen maid but she is dead now. My brother, Paco, is dead too. He was a communist. He sang such lovely songs."

"So many people are dead now."

"Silly! Everybody dies."

"Why?"

"What do you mean why?"

"Why? That's all."

She shrugged her shoulders.

"Have you any money?"

"I think . . . Yes, I have money."

"Buy me a drink."

He called the waiter.

"You're very pale. Are you sick?"

"No."

"What is your name?"

"My name?" He began to scratch his head desperately. "My name? Oh, yes, André. Certainly, André."

"Are you French?"

"Your hair must have been so lovely."

"Naughty boy! You have had too much to drink. Give me a cigarette."

He took an envelope out of his pocket. His movements were measured, slow, as he no longer counted on even the simplest of his reactions. He stared at the envelope, trying to remember, trying to think. But there was a constant booming in his head, and that made it difficult.

The envelope was filled with bills. He took out a five-hundred peseta note and handed it to her. "Here, buy cigarettes."

She glanced at the contents of the envelope and she was startled because she had never seen so much money. He must be a very great gentleman, she thought, to have so much money.

"Who are you?"

"I'm a sailor. No, I'm not a sailor."

"Be careful with the money."

"What's that you've got under your arm?"

She showed him the photo album.

"Have you a photo you could give me?" she said. "I keep photos of all the men I have known. Often in the morning I'm alone in bed and it is frightening, so I look at my album for hours. Do you think I'm silly? Sometimes I talk to my photos."

"No. It's not silly."

"It is so good," she said. "If only it was good all the time."

He kissed her hand. She withdrew it hastily.

"Many of them are signed. Later, up in my room, I'll show you."

He blinked. There was something important that he had to do. What? "May I touch your hair?" he asked.

"Don't be bad! We'll soon go up to my room." She squeezed his hand. "Then you can do everything. I'm very good. All the men say so."

Unconsciously he reached out and caught a lock of hair between his shaky fingers. She tossed her head back, her hair swirling about, falling again to her shoulders. He sensed the nature of his rejection, he slumped back in his chair. The girl sneered. At nineteen she had already grasped that her silken hair was hoax and that the only truth was to make herself eager many times nightly so that faceless men might enjoy her again and again.

"Who is that man sitting there?"

"I don't know."

The man – a tall, balding German – heard, and shifted in his chair.

"He must be a foreigner." So many things, he thought. Why can't I remember?

She took him by the hand. "Come, we'll go to my room. We'll have fun."

It was damp outside, and still misty. But the fresh air was exhilarating.

"If I'm good will you tip well?"

"Did you see if the man got up?"

"The man! Phew! I'll do anything you want. So long as you pay."

"That's not what I meant."

"Don't be shy *guapo*."

The room was small. A rope was suspended from one cracked wall to the other. Two soiled towels and a faded pink slip hung from a rope. A small, unscreened window looked out on the street. A bottle of wine, a package of cheese, and an ashtray overflowing with butts were on the window-sill.

He flopped down on the bed.

"Are there any rats?"

"No."

She was at the sink, filling up a pail of water.

"I want to go . . ."

"Now you be good!"

"I don't want to pay. I want to make love for nothing."

"But you have so much money."

"I don't want to pay."

She laughed. "You try to sleep while I get ready," she said.

He felt the tiny sensation of sharp claws creeping along his trouser leg. On his thigh now, slowly, moving stealthily. He opened his eyes. And there, sniffing along his thigh, now almost on his stomach, was a rat. *Suddenly something snapped, he felt it go.* The strain, the booming in his head, everything easing up. So they *were* wrong. The doctors, Chaim, Pepe, they were all wrong. There were, and always had been, rats in the room. He wanted to sing or dance or cry. But he was careful not to move, not to startle the animal, he watched it crawl, cautious, grey, up his body. It stopped on his chest. Suddenly, from different directions, he shot both his hands out at the rat.

Sweating, he lay there, clutching his rumpled shirt, digging his fingernails into his own skin.

He screamed.

"Stop it!" Lolita grabbed her hair and pulled at it as if she would go crazy. "Do you want me to be thrown out of here too?"

He stared at her dumbly. He was deeply puzzled, but he was not certain about what.

"Don't be greedy," she said. "I'll only be a minute. But I'm not going to undress you as well. Now off with your clothes *guapo!*"

She flung her kimono to the floor.

Her body was olive, rounded, and warm-looking. As though suspended in a mood she could not comprehend she walked towards him slowly. She seemed to be saying with her body, if you just give me a chance, just a bit of a chance, I can make it right. He watched in amazement. Time seemed to stop, waiting on her, allowing her a chance at self-redemption. And then suddenly, as if she perceived the irony of the situation, she relapsed into vulgarity. Smiling, giggling moronically, she paused immediately before him. She rubbed her arms and brushed back her hair, her eyes widening. "Good!" she said in English. "Spaneeesh one."

"I'm sorry. Please forgive me," he said. He jumped off the bed and grabbed her in his arms. "I'm sorry."

She pushed him away. "Take your clothes off!"

"I can't. I don't want to."

"Hurry!"

"No, please, no."

"Then pay me. You wasted my time. Pay me now!"

He shuddered, and laughing, he grabbed her in his arms. "I'm not going to fight him. No, not at all! I don't understand, but I'm beginning to. It's coming. No, I'm not going to fight him. I'm going to live. I'm going to get her now. I do love her. Yes, I do."

"Give me my money!"

He pulled the envelope out of his pocket. Holding it high, he overturned it. Money spiralling, tumbling, falling to the floor. She fell down on her hands and knees and began snatching up the notes.

"It's no good," he said. "Don't pick it up."

But she had not heard him. She was sprawled out on the floor, naked, gathering up the notes quickly.

"I'm free," he stumbled absently. "I don't understand, but ..."

He left the room, stepping over her, and she hardly noticed.

XII

Suddenly all the street lights were extinguished and the fireworks display began.

A thin nervous line of red light shot up into the sky, ripping the darkness, exploding into shivering streaks of red and orange and green. Another scratch of light darted skywards, shattering itself in mid-air and momentarily illuminating the plaza in an eerie yellow. The people sighed ominously. Some recoiling, others tittering. Soon the sky was exploded in a multi-coloured grandeur, bleeding a myriad of trickling starlets, shot through with gaping holes and oblique pin-lines of firecracker lights.

A man in the crowd fell into a fit of laughter.

The giant *falla* of the wooden gypsy burst into flames. The crowd gasped. They trembled.

Another send-off of rocket lights swooshed into the sky, blossoming open above the flames of the burning *falla*, spluttering and hissing, pumping more angry rents into the sky.

An elderly woman, quivering, clutched Toni by the arm.

Still another flurry zoomed heavenwards, rattling, spluttering, dribbling coloured stars on the plaza.

XIII

He heard the first of the explosions, he saw the lights in the sky, all around him minor *fallas* were going up in flames.

He saw Kraus as well, but he did not pay any attention.

He walked across to the bridge still feeling puzzled about some things but richly resolved about others. The bridge, the dead river, the madly lit sky, all seemed wonderfully good. He stood silently for a moment, feeling amazed with himself, remembering that somehow it had started in the room. But he remembered nothing in particular, no incident, no idea, just a vague kind of pain. A duty, perhaps. Something, anyway, that he had undertaken long ago. The duty itself was unremembered, but the need to act, the dignity that was truly wanted, came through clearly.

First off, they would have to get back to Canada. There had been enough of this, now he had work to do. He would work with what he knew, that would have to do. Jesus, he wanted to talk to her!

Below, on the river bed, a group of men were huddled around a twig fire. André felt that he wanted to join them. It would be just fine to tell them how he felt or maybe joke about women and the system. I am a bigger man now, he thought. My feelings are more than anger. His laugh began slowly then swelled up and broke out happily. But he was not yet certain what was happening to him. It will take time, he thought.

Kraus put a hand on his shoulder and whirled him around. "What are you laughing at?" he asked.

André started. "Kraus. Roger Kraus."

Kraus snatched his hand away. He saw André's face wild and drunk and brilliant in the quick light of an exploding *falla*. He was suspicious of the way André had used his name. He had made it sound as if there was some doubt about whether he was Roger Kraus or not.

André laughed again.

Kraus moved back quickly and felt a hard knot of something form in his stomach. "Why are you always laughing?"

André grinned, trying to be reassuring. "I'm fine. Honest I am," he said. "You know, I feel like working. I'm going back to my room to paint."

Kraus stood in his way.

"What's wrong?" André asked hoarsely. "What do you want?"

Kraus cocked his head to a side, incredulously. "Don't you remember? Are you mad?"

André passed his hand over his forehead. He felt dazed. But I'm not mad, he thought. "Remember what?"

"You said that you were going to kill me."

André looked hard at Kraus and he remembered him or thought he remembered him striking old Mr. Blumberg. He remembered him in bed with Toni (while he himself, André, sat stupid in a chair, listening to time passing) or Ida who was dead, his filth inside her. (In that chair, rocking on a cloud perhaps, being unused and unknown.) Yes, it was Kraus. It had been Kraus always. "I don't know. I – I seem to remember so many things. I don't . . ." What if he is stronger than I am, he thought? What if he should kill me? Right now, when it is beginning. "Why have you been following me?"

"You were unfaithful to her," Kraus said vehemently, and as if by saying it he had put everything right. "You went up to the room with the whore. I saw you."

"Did you see the girl? She had . . ." No, André thought. He wouldn't understand if I told him about her hair. "What business is it of yours?"

Kraus said nothing. He was growing anxious. Always, they wanted to talk. Why couldn't they get it over with?

André tried to walk past him but Kraus stood in his way again. "I thought you were going to kill me," he said.

"I was, but . . ." But there was Toni. Painting. Chaim. "It would be stupid to die this way."

"You are afraid."

So that's it, André thought. All I have to say is that I'm afraid. And God knows I am. *But I am other things too.*

Suddenly André seized him by the collar. "Look, I'm afraid, is that okay? Christ, I don't want to die now. It would . . ."

Kraus stamped his foot. His face was red. His eyes were wet. "I can't stand you," he said. "You – you won't let me alone. You, why do you look at me?" And then, panting, he pulled back and smashed André in the ribs.

André wobbled. He gaped, trying to suck in air.

Kraus watched, not knowing what to do. His eyes bulged.

And just before he struck out at him, André noticed the men around the fire again, and he thought: Now, I will never joke with them. His punch caught Kraus on the nose.

André knew it was wrong. He knew that he should not have wasted that first punch. But it was his face that was so ugly.

XIV

Then nothing.

Stillness.

The plaza was lost in a fog of fumes. The old woman had disappeared from Toni's side.

Where is he right now, Toni thought? I knew that morning on the river. Strange, it seemed years ago now, long ago and in a different country, when they had still been young and still been foolish. Actually, all they had had together had been an exciting weekend.

The doomed gypsy, burning, leered from within the yellow gloom. The crowd backed further and further away. Suddenly, the gypsy's belly – which had been packed with firecrackers – exploded. The sky went up in flames.

Somewhere, she hoped he was watching. She knew he had always wanted to see it burn. She knew, that if he saw, it would make it easier for him.

XV

André was watching all right.

Lying face upwards, half on the grass and half in the mud, he was watching the burning sky which was full of winking and exploding stars, real and unreal. He was watching the sky swinging around the bridge or the bridge rocking against the sky. *Toni, I want you to know that I was afraid and that I told him.*

The ground was sinking away from him. He felt that it was improper for he was lying flat on it, but the ground was sinking away from him as if he was going up and away from it in an elevator. *Toni, don't you be afraid.* He gasped. His breath was sporadic and his mouth was warm and thick with blood. *If the men by the fire hear me and come to me, I wonder what I will tell them?*

He was not certain whether he was still in his room or with Toni or Chaim or hitting Mr. Blumberg.

I will tell them yes and ask for a cigarette. It's not much to ask for if you're dying. I've given away quite a few myself in my day. Now I'm urinating, he thought. Usually I would think now I'm pissing or having a leak. But dying is very medical.

He wanted to roll over because he felt that the jagged end of a rock was in his back. But he could not move himself. Or he did move himself and his body did not go with him. *Yes, that's funny. I must tell Chaim. I mean watching yourself going like this and thinking about your own thoughts while they're going on.* My mother will say that I passed away. She is afraid of the word death.

He felt a lump in his throat, but only dimly as consciousness was slipping from him. He was sobbing. *No. No. All I ask is that I know what's going on. That's all. Never mind the cigarette. Just knowing, eh. Or feeling.*

In grade six B listen now Miss Crankshaw had read Toni from a book which said do not move injured bodies you know until an MD arrives yes even if it is raining catsanddogs snow burning *falla* and one fine day she asked me André saying it Anne-dree what please is the capital of Poland O Apoo visiting princess lovely of my dreams and I couldn't answer for I was intent on the hairy thing on her cheek which was colour ugly *if I feel tomorrow* so 8¼ years later on I joked with Collins *if you don like my apples* no I never stuffed Miss C oh God no ugly like father saying that's filthy or Serge hugging me saying don't tell please don't God no but *why do you shake my tree* not Jean-Paul who was alright when my father says there is no second best in war or business oh stop this ohgoddingno crap you dont believe in it for ½ second no you don't (now there is a man standing over me) and mama saying now still I bet do not leave me ever in the dark not ugly the girl's hair or the sun at oh Apoo on the église in French of St. Germain-des-Prés or Toni o my love I didn't did I mean tell him I was afraid her breasts dipping full (the man is waiting for me to die) why doesn't the sky stay still for one just one second eh but I do not want to die with my eyes open not closing like Ida in my dreams o

"Oh."

Suddenly, his fists digging into the mud, he pulled himself upwards. He thought he was screaming but his voice was small. "No. Just a bit – yet."

Then he fell backwards, his face in the mud.

His eyes remained open, but the man saw that he was dead and he walked away.

BOOK FOUR

A T 3 A.M. Barney staggered up to the room again to see if she was in. Jessie was lying in bed, smoking, and sipping gin. Barney nodded shyly.

"Hello," he said.

"Thanks for the flowers."

He noticed the flowers, slightly wilted, lying at the foot of the bed.

"Well, where were you?" he asked.

"I beg your pardon?"

"You had quite a bit to drink last night."

"Oh, stop it! My head is bursting."

"Her head is bursting."

She smiled wryly. "Evidently I didn't have enough to please you," she said.

"Just what do you mean by that?"

"Did you get to the brothel last night, honey-bunny? Regardless of the fact that you are the father of two small children, regardless of the fact that you might have contracted some dreadful disease and infected me."

"I found you here kissing that tramp!"

"I'm not deaf!"

She had half-forgotten André. Now she remembered him tenderly, so that she felt a need to protect him. A joyful need that having an unloved man's children had never given her. "We were both drunk," she said. "It meant nothing."

"What did you expect me to think?"

"I didn't expect you to think anything."

"Put yourself in my place I mean . . ."

"Oh Barney, stop being a child."

He winced. He tried not to reel.

"What did we want to come to Europe for?" he said. "Let's go home. I'll buy you a convertible."

"Thanks, honey-bunny. But I'm too old for toys. In fact, I've been doing some thinking. I want to be loved. I'm tired of this."

She climbed lazily out of bed. Long-legged, slim, smiling trimly, she might easily have stepped out of any number of popular cigarette ads. She stretched, yawned, and brushed ashes off her black lace nightgown.

Barney grabbed her roughly. "Gimme a kiss, baby," he said.

She pushed him away easily, and then she laughed. "Why, Barney, you're drunk!" she cried.

"Sure, I'm drunk. Why not? Kmir baby!"

"Oh, don't be foolish. You're a grown man."

He grabbed her again. Her mouth was cold, unopened. He was drunk, still he shivered. She tried to push him away but he clung to her stubbornly. They fell down on the bed. He squeezed her to him and she began to struggle. He was breathing in short puffs. He was hurting her. With a great shove she managed to break away. She slapped him across the face and jumped off the bed.

"Darn you!"

Barney sat up. "You wouldnta moved away so quick if it was André, huh? You would have been crazy for that pinch coming from him!"

He got up unsteadily and walked towards her.

"André? Don't be an idiot!"

"I know all about the others too, *honey-bunny!* There's a name for women like you."

She laughed, her lips quivering. "You never had it to give to me. Never! Impotent fool!"

He slapped her.

"Impotent!"

He slapped her again.

"Slut!"

And suddenly he turned away, and he was sick.

He collapsed on the edge of the bed. His head hanging between his knees he was sick again and again. He felt his eyes popping, sweat soaking him, and his nose stinging. Staring downwards dreamily – his head hanging limply, jerking alive again as his whole body shook in another fit of vomiting – all he could see was his own spew. Finally, he had no more to bring up. He lay back on the bed exhausted. He felt an odd sensation of wellbeing flutter through him.

When she believed that he had rested enough, Jessie brought him a glass of cold water. He drank it slowly. He wanted to lie there for ever. Jessie lit a cigarette and slipped it between her lips.

"Feeling better?"

He took a long puff of his cigarette. She was seated on the edge of the bed. So calm, so unruffled. He envied her.

"You married me for my money, didn't you?" he asked.

"Yes."

"And you hate me because I'm a Jew?"

"No, I don't hate you."

"Derek says you hate me."

"How does Derek come into this?"

"Do you think it was fair?"

"No."

"No. She doesn't think it was fair."

His voice was breaking. She did not want to see what was coming.

"I was very young," she said. "I got my notice a short while before I met you. You could give me all the things I wanted.

I'm sorry, it was a mistake. But you didn't really love me either, Barney."

"I suppose I bought you with my money?"

"Yes."

He laughed. "I worked so hard to make my money."

"Do you want a divorce?"

"Divorce?" he said, his voice trembling.

"We might as well face it."

He rolled over in bed so that she could not see his face or that his eyes were wet. "Always giving me the shit about the business, about how I skimped and saved. But it was good enough to buy you clothes and stuff, huh? Good enough to pay off the bums you hung around with? All that crap about your family. You didn't marry below yourself. Your father was a crook. A crook, do you hear? Don't worry, I know. I know a lot of things. My father may have been poor but let me tell you we paid our bills. We never took anything from anybody. Not even a crumb of bread if we were starving. So I'm a Jew, huh? Go ahead, tell me. I changed my name. Well, I was wrong. I only wish I was a rabbi or something, then I'd tell you. I'd quote facts. Just look at the job we're doing in Israel! I was talking to a guy only . . ."

"I'm going out for a walk," she said.

He started to get up. "Wait. I'm sorry. I'll go with you."

"I'll see you later," she said. "Don't worry, I'm not angry. I just want to be alone for a few moments."

He watched her go.

"Were you serious about the divorce?"

"I don't know. I'm not sure."

She's going to André, he thought. He comes from a good family, he's not a Jew.

Barney lay back on the bed and pushed the flowers away with his foot.

II

Seated at the bar in the Tango Club, Derek grinned tipsily at a brawny man who he thought was definitely gay. The man moved away and Juanito edged in beside Derek.

"You're late," Derek said.

"I'm sorry. I got away as soon as I could."

"Well?"

"You were right," Juanito said. "André has disappeared. He probably left with the Jew."

"Splendid, D.J. What are you going to do about it?"

"Nothing. He is my friend." Juanito felt he was an important figure now that André had disappeared. Many people stopped him to ask for news of André, and always Juanito shrugged his shoulders, as if he knew but could not say. Toni, naturally, believed he was dead. But that, Juanito thought, was only because she couldn't imagine him leaving her. "André is crazy," Juanito said. "Imagine him running off only because of two hundred dollars. I can't understand it."

Derek laughed. "You're priceless, D.J.," he said.

"I did the best I could for him, but I never got so much as a word of thanks. He betrayed me for money! Have you any news from your sister and brother-in-law?"

The fiesta was over. Only the habitual drinkers idled about the bar. They were as pleased as children at a fair that their wonderland was their very own again, but there was one intruder to mar the gaiety of the reunion. A jolly man, who had missed his train to Madrid again, was guzzling champagne all by himself. He made the occasional announcement. His last one had been to the effect that he was more irresistible to women than anyone else in the Club. Then, his own laughter consumed him.

"They're still here," Derek said. "Jessie says that Barney is acting very strangely. He's talking about going to Israel with the children. But don't worry, they'll make up again. How long has André been missing?"

"He didn't show up at his hotel Monday night. It's odd, he left all his things there."

"Perhaps he's gone off into the mountains to contemplate his navel?"

"Toni believes that he is dead."

"Who's Toni?"

"She's his mistress." Juanito noticed that Luís was watching them. He averted his eyes. "She says that we killed him and that he is in the river." Juanito did not mention Guillermo to Derek. He did not want Derek to know that he had been questioned and insulted. He tapped his forehead and shrugged his shoulders. "You know how it is?"

"Oh shettup!" Derek said quickly.

Derek was angry. The past could not be truly erased. It was there, a shape in the darkness, lurking there always, waiting to leap up at him. He did not have the strength to resist Juanito or the love to help Barney but his heart still went out to André and the others.

Juanito flushed. "If you talk to me like that I will . . ."

"All right. I'm sorry." He laughed. "If you only knew how sorry, D.J."

Luís leaned over the bar towards Juanito. His eyes were hot and melancholy. "Why couldn't you have told Guillermo what you knew?" he asked. "André was your friend."

Derek turned to Juanito. "What does he want?"

"He's a friend of André's. He used to work for Chaim in the Mocambo Club."

"It doesn't matter," Luís said. "Guillermo knows. Ask Kraus if he doesn't know? Ask his sister?"

Juanito pushed Luís away. "You're drunk."

Luís trembled. "It's his sister. She's mad, I tell you. She . . ." He giggled. "She's ugly."

The man who had missed his train to Madrid called for another bottle of champagne, and Luís moved away sadly.

Juanito laughed nervously.

"What goes on between you and the German colonel?" Derek asked quickly.

"Are you crazy? What do you think I am?"

Derek patted Juanito's cheek.

"Don't do that here!"

"What about you and the gorgeous German?"

"Nothing!"

Derek looked around, but the German was nowhere in sight. Still, he was jealous. He required, as always, constant confirmations of love. "I got you a gift," he said. "Here you are."

It was a gold cigarette case. The initial J had been engraved on it.

Juanito pressed Derek's hand. "Thank you. It is very beautiful."

"Tell me that you love me."

"Here?"

"They don't understand English!"

"But I . . ."

"Quick!"

"I love you."

The man at the bar got his bottle of champagne. He said, in a booming voice: "*Olé! Vivan los maricones! Arriba!*"

"Shall we go?" Derek asked.

"Did you, I mean for my friend . . ."

"I brought you the money."

"Let me finish my cognac, and we'll go."

Derek waited.

"Will you take me to America?"

"Of course, darling."

And why not, Juanito thought? I am a Spanish gentleman and in America there are many wealthy ladies. If André can steal, why can't I do this? It was very common among the great men of Rome.

"Hurry!"

"You promised to arrange everything. Papers, passage."

Derek laughed. He raised his glass. "*Vivan los maricones!*" he said.

The man roared. His stomach shook. "*Viva!*"

III

"Get more twigs. The fire is going out."

"The fire is *not* going out."

"López has caught a frog. He wants to put it in the soup."

López grinned boyishly and knocked a bit of ash off his new shirt. The sleeves were too long. They hung down over his wrists.

"Sometimes your jokes aren't so funny, López."

"The French eat frogs."

"To hell with the frog! When is the soup going to be ready?"

All five of them were huddled around the tiny twig fire underneath the bridge. Juan, their leader, stirred the soup. The others held on to their tin-cans impatiently. The ground was damp.

"We have two new tenants tonight."

Ortega giggled. "Send around the manager to ask them for their marriage licence."

"I'm hungry!"

"How can you talk of food in a time of crisis?"

"Do you want our hotel getting a bad reputation?"

A car shot across the bridge. They sat silently until it passed.

"Are you afraid?"

"You can never tell."

"It would not look so good for you, eh?"

"Aren't you wearing his shoes?"

Old José, seated slightly apart from the others, shook his head. "It was wrong. A catastrophe is going to happen. I can feel it."

"Quiet, you old fool!"

"What? Is God going to punish us?"

Renato laughed over-enthusiastically.

"No, not God. Man will punish us. We have sinned against man. That is dreadful."

López made a sign of the cross. "Forgive me, Saint José."

"Enough of this," Juan said authoritatively. "Are you a bunch of old women?"

"Ruíz is worried about the body."

"Body?"

"Who saw a body?"

"We have done a dreadful thing."

"Shettup!"

"Wasn't he rich?"

"It does not matter what he was."

"Your two sons died in the war and now you worry about fascists."

"My sons died so that things might be different."

"Go ahead, tell us they died for the fascists."

"The fascists are to be pitied. They do not know what they are doing."

"They will suffer in the next world, eh?"

López howled with laughter.

"When they shot Julio it did not matter that they did not know what they were doing. They shot him and he is dead."

"But we can't go on this way. Don't you understand?"

"We were just being kind. We thought he would be more comfortable in the cave."

"Poor lad."

"Sh!"

A small, worried man stepped out of the shadows. They knew him and they knew what he represented. Sometimes he gave them pamphlets to read. Often he came with others, and they passed out sandwiches, clothes.

"*Buenas noches*, Guillermo."

"*Salud!*"

"Would you like some soup?"

"No."

Juan smiled thinly. "We haven't seen you for a long time," he said.

"I've been away."

"How long have you been standing in the shadows?"

Guillermo sat down on the grass and lit a cigarette. He noticed Ortega's shoes, but he said nothing.

"Have you been here long?"

"About ten minutes."

Renato wandered around behind Guillermo.

"Sit down, Renato. Don't be a fool," Guillermo said quietly, his eyes brilliant and cold in the flickering light.

"I was just going for a walk."

"Sit down!"

"Have you brought us any pamphlets?"

"I read the last one from cover to cover."

"What did you do with the body?"

Juan looked blank. The men looked down at the ground.

"I want to see that he is properly buried."

Juan stopped stirring the soup. "We know of no body," he said.

Guillermo seized López by the collar. He pushed him up against the concrete wall and shook him back and forth. "It takes much courage and nobility to steal a shirt from a dead man," he said. "Doesn't it, comrade López?"

He let him go.

"We did not kill him."

"I know."

"He was dead when we found him."

"It would have been better if we had killed him," José said, "but to find him dead, another man, and . . ."

"What need had he of such fine clothes?"

"We are poor, honest men. You are supposed to protect us."

"Where is the body?"

"In the cave."

"I'll be right back. Don't any of you go away. Juan, I'm holding you responsible."

They waited until Guillermo had disappeared into the darkness.

"Where would we go?"

The cave was dark and damp, moisture dripped from the walls. André lay naked on the ground. Not quite naked, for there were newspapers strewn about him. There were bruises on his chest and his abdomen had turned a sort of greenish-yellow in colour. His body smelled sweet and putrid. Guillermo was sweating and he had gritted his teeth. He lit a match, and looking into André's face he saw that his eyes were drying and shrinking back into his skull. They were cloudy. His facial skin was grey and his mouth was shut. His expression was not angry or surprised or benign. It was exhausted but still somewhat eager. As if he was waiting for something which had not yet arrived but could be expected shortly, an abysmal something perhaps.

But Guillermo could only guess.

And guessing, he sighed also. He felt weak and discouraged. I'm not used to it yet, he thought. I wonder how many more times I will have to see it before I can get used to it?

Toni will be difficult, he thought. She will want to see him. He turned away from André. It is too bad that the Colonel's sister has seen me so often, he thought. She knows that I am watching the house. That will also mean difficulties.

Ortega waved a lead pipe in the air. It was the first pair of shoes he had owned in eleven years. They fit well. "He is alone," he said. "Just say the word, Juan."

"Throw away the pipe!"

Renato spit. "He will have a fine job talking me out of the pants."

"There will be a catastrophe. We have broken faith."

"Quiet!"

Guillermo was pale. He held a handkerchief to his nose. "I thought that he would need a shave," he said.

"Did you know him?"

"I want three men. I'll get shovels. We are going to bury him in the cave."

"It stinks in there!"

"I'll come, if you like?"

"Have some soup first," Guillermo said, sitting down. "Juan, have you any coffee?"

"Have some soup. It's hot."

"Do we have to return the clothes?"

Guillermo sighed. "I'll leave it up to you," he said.

"I'm keeping the pants. He doesn't need them."

Guillermo accepted a tin of soup. It was hot. He did not want the men to see that he was shivering.

"What happened?" Guillermo asked.

"López saw."

López laughed nervously.

"Well?"

"There were two men fighting on the bridge." He got up and pointed. "They had been fighting for some time. The dead man was taking a bad beating. He got up again and again. Finally the other man threw him over. It was about one o'clock. I know the time because just as he fell over I heard the noise of the big *falla* exploding."

"Was he still alive?"

"He was groaning something awful. But only for a short time."

"Why didn't you go over to him?"

"Do you think I'm a fool. They would say that I killed him."

"López is right. It is not as if he was a comrade."

"He was a foreigner."

Guillermo lit a cigarette. He passed around the pack. "We are all comrades. Do you understand?"

"Was he a friend of yours?"

"He was a friend to all of us."

"How were we to know?"

Guillermo shivered. He felt deeply ashamed of himself.

"What did the other man look like, López?"

"I couldn't see him very well. But he was tall."

"Did you hear him say anything?"

"I couldn't understand. It wasn't Spanish."

Guillermo waited until Juan poured the soup for the men.

"You see, Guillermo. You can do nothing. Bad is bad."

"You are much too cynical, José." Guillermo turned to the others. "I'll be back in fifteen minutes. I'll bring coffee and cigarettes. Don't go away."

"Do we have to bury him?"

"Yes."

"Do we have to return the clothes?"

"He doesn't need the shoes. He is not going to walk away."

"You may keep the clothes," Guillermo said. In the flickering light he searched for José's face. "What would you give them, old man? What would you do?"

"I don't know."

Guillermo said nothing.

"I wish I knew," José said. "Mercy, perhaps . . ."

"You cannot eat mercy."

IV

She was dressed as if ready to go out. If her arms had not been hanging limply from her shoulders, if one of them had been raised and pointed towards the door, she might have been making an absurd face at someone. She had never been an attractive woman, but now hanging from the dining-room chandelier she seemed longer and thinner than she had ever really been. Her head, tilted slightly forward, fell to her shoulder. Her tongue hung dumbly from her mouth. The chair, the one she usually sat on, had been kicked over. She had hanged herself with his old skipping rope, the one he had used when he was in training for the Olympics.

When he had first entered the room he had shuddered, but that had been shock. Now he eyed her with repugnant interest. He walked around her and around her. At last he was able to study her without fear. He poked her in the ribs, and she swung back towards him, hitting him on the shoulder.

He read the note again.

Roger,

I told you I was going away. Now what will you do? Little, wooden soldier.

You killed the boy out of jealousy and now they will get you. I'll wager that even now the small man is waiting by the window. Go, go, have a look. Idiot!

I never believed in it – never! It was all because of him.

Theresa Kraus Ph.D.

He had never learned how to disobey or question her so he walked over to the window almost automatically. The small, worried man, Guillermo, was still there. Another man was talking to him.

Yes, Theresa had told him about Guillermo. She had first seen him waiting by the lamp post across the street on Tuesday night. Immediately, she had been suspicious. So

Kraus had checked with Maríano and had discovered that Guillermo was a suspected communist. But Maríano had done nothing about it, and this made the fifth night that Guillermo had passed by and stood sullenly by the lamp post.

Roger studied his sister blankly. He did not know what to do next. He was a puppet and he had suddenly been cut down from his strings. Should he dance? Collapse? He tried hard to think. Reflexes, emotions, reactions. But nothing dignified by either the logical or the intellectual.

"I killed him for you. You made me kill him. You made me kill all of them."

The boy had fought stupidly.

Once, Kraus remembered, when the boy had fallen down again, he had thought: All right. He has had his lesson.

But somehow the boy had managed to scramble to his feet again. And even then Kraus would have let him go. But it was the expression on the boy's face that had settled it, an expression not so much superior as triumphant and composed. He had – and Kraus still did not know how – conveyed to him that he was ugly and didn't matter. So in a moment of rage Kraus had picked him up and heaved him over the bridge.

He had felt compelled to do so. Just as he had felt compelled to climb down after him and watch him die.

He remembered that Theresa had been jubilant. He had entered the house quietly and she had had only one look at him when she had said: "You have killed the artist." And then she had laughed in the same way she had laughed when she had said: "It doesn't matter." But she had refused to listen to the details. She had said: "At last we are equal. I don't want to hear one detail. I want you to keep it."

He had not understood what she had meant by that.

Why? Why did they go on fighting? You killed one, and another came along! An endless parade of angry men. Why did they go on fighting? Didn't they know?

"Why?"

The corpse stared back at him dumbly. The eyes were bulging.

"What would you have said had it been me who had committed suicide?"

He climbed up on a chair and shut her eyes. Then maliciously, he ripped open her blouse. Her breasts horrified him. He jumped down from the chair. The left eye refused to remain shut. It stared.

"It's a lie. You believed. You always believed."

He poked her, timidly at first, then he punched her solidly in the stomach. She swung upwards, backwards, crashing down to the floor. The chandelier swung madly.

"I have to believe."

He thought he heard a noise at the door. He rushed downstairs and fastened the bolts. He drew all the window shades. He locked the back door. Then, when everything had been attended to, he sat down on a chair in his own room, his Mauser on his lap, sweating.

"What will I do?"

V

"Are you coming to the meeting?"

"I don't know."

"You are supposed to give a report on the activities of our comrades from Barcelona."

"I'll come along later."

Manuel cupped his hand and lit a match. His hollow cheeks flared in the brief light. "You are an idiot, Guillermo."

"Look! He just drew the blind."

"Are you going to kill him?"

"Yes."

"Doubtlessly they will shoot you, doubtlessly they will exploit the incident to round up ten or twenty comrades, doubtlessly they . . ."

"All right! I know."

"Look, he was not murdered. He committed suicide."

"Wasn't he thrown off the bridge?"

"That has nothing to do with it."

"You did not know him like I did."

"I met him once. He committed suicide."

"I would like to revenge his murder."

"That's a very pretty thought."

"He was in love with a girl here. He was such a damn good painter."

"In prison there are many men. Some of them married, some of them with children. I'm going now. I'm going to ask that you be expelled. You are too romantic for this kind of work. It would be dangerous to trust you with further responsibilities."

"If it was you what would you do?"

"Nothing. I would feel nothing. We can't afford it."

"It's difficult."

"Are you coming?"

"I guess so."

They walked for a bit, then Guillermo stopped. He said: "Manuel, it is going to be beautiful!"

"Let go of my collar!"

"All this is not for nothing!"

"Yes. It is going to be beautiful."

VI

The baby was wailing again, and soon María would have to be fed. Luís poured the coffee into the cup, laboriously checking so that it would not overflow, and then he carried it in to her.

"You are so good, Luís."

He laughed. Her gratitude embarrassed him. "Drink the coffee," he said. "It's hot."

She held her hand to her mouth and coughed. She accepted the cup gratefully.

He did not own a bed so he had prepared a mattress for her on the floor. All morning he had hunted for coal and in the late afternoon he had returned and prepared a coal fire for her in the basin. Now the basin, glowing warmly, was beside her on the floor. The room was small, the paper on the walls was peeling. Old crates served as dressers, cupboards, and a table. On the wall, hanging very conspicuously, was André's picture, the unfinished nude. Luís had liked the picture very much, and just to surprise María he had mended the tear with a string and hung it on the wall while she was dozing.

"Is the baby sleeping?"

"Yes," he said.

"I hear him crying. Bring him to me."

He brought her the baby. He was wrapped in several towels, and bawling.

"I'll hold him until you finish your coffee."

He rocked the baby to and fro in his arms. He felt awkward, ashamed also. He tried hard to visualise the baby as some day being a man but he could not see it.

"You are funny with the baby."

He smiled sternly. He had meant to laugh, but Toni was huddled on a pillow in a corner of the room and her presence had inhibited him. Her eyes were sad and moist. Her face had in it a new quality of pain or maturity and she was huddled in such a way that it seemed her intention was to repudiate the beauty of her body.

Toni had stayed up most of the night waiting for Guillermo. She had not heard from him since he had said that he was going down to the river, and that had been two days ago.

"You will make a good father," María said. "Here, give him to his mother."

He lay the baby down beside her. He was so wrinkled and pink. Luís thought he was very ugly.

"Little Jeem André José Villian-Rodríguez."

"I saw him today," Luís said. He smiled at Toni and Toni smiled back at him.

"When?" María asked.

"This afternoon, in Cosmi's."

"Was he sober?"

"Well he wasn't drunk. I mean he looked much better."

"Did you tell him about the child?"

"Yes. I also told him that you were staying here with me."

"What did he say?"

"He feels badly about not having a job. He, I think he's sick. I told him, I said, you have a son. I knew it would be a boy, he said. But the expression on his face never changed. Aren't you pleased? I said. Why should I be pleased? he said. If he is any good they will get him like they got the others. And if he is going to be bad I do not want him."

"Is he coming home?"

"He didn't say. We had a long talk though."

"Yes?"

"I couldn't understand most of it. All that talk about harmonicas! I don't think he has eaten a meal since he found out. Why is it always the good ones, again and again, he said that to me. I tried to reason with him. I told him that if a man thinks too much he goes crazy. Why? Why? All the time he wants to know why."

"You are a good friend to him."

Luís grinned shyly. "We fought together."

Luís had also told Pepe about how troubled he had been ever since that afternoon in Fräulein Kraus's house. He had told him that the only reason why he had not made love to her that day had been that she was ugly, and that had worried him so much that he had hardly slept since that day.

Suddenly Luís remembered something. He turned to Toni. "André once told me that politics didn't interest him as such. He said it was poverty that was ugly, and that so-called justice was beside the point. He said that the poor must have more because they were human and no human should be ugly."

Toni smiled. "It's all right," she said. "I was in love with him. I like it when you talk about him."

"Does Pepe still not believe that he committed suicide?" María asked.

"He says André would never do it."

"Poor Pepe."

"They arrested most of the gang. It looks bad for them. They were wearing his clothes. There were bruises on the body."

"They didn't kill him," Toni said.

"What do you think, María?"

"I do not think. I pray."

"Do you pray for Pepe?"

"Yes."

Luís laughed. So did Toni.

"Why is it funny?"

"Does he know?"

"No."

"I should tell him. That would make him laugh."

Pepe entered the room very quietly and they did not hear him come in. His eyes were red and his lips were dry, but he was sober and he had shaved and shined his shoes.

"Pepe!"

"They got Guillermo before I even got a chance to talk to him."

Toni bit her lip. She squeezed her belly in anger. I will kill him, she thought. I will invite him up to my room and stab him.

"What's the charge?" Luís asked.

"Barcelona. Also, they know about his pamphlets."

"But he is usually so careful. How did they get him?"

"It was an accident. There was a meeting but it had been called off. Guillermo didn't know, he hadn't seen the others. He arrived late with another man and they were both arrested."

"He's a good man."

"Yes." Pepe turned to Toni. "There is a special letter for you at Cosmi's. It's from Chaim. Cosmi got word to him."

Luís got up. "Come, Toni. We'll go to Cosmi's."

Toni looked as if she was going to protest. Her face was hot with grief. She grabbed her belly. "I . . ." She stopped short. "He had no skin. Only blood!"

Luís helped her up. She looked at him imploringly and he blushed. "I don't know what to say," he said.

She kissed him. "You are good, Luís. You . . ."

Pepe turned to Luís. "Bring her right back. She'll eat with us. Chaim is making arrangements. Meanwhile . . . Well, bring her right back."

Luís nodded. "Until later," he said.

As soon as they had left, Pepe laughed nervously.

"How are you?" María asked.

"All right. And you?"

"All right."

"It is very hot again," he said.

"Isn't that one of his pictures?"

"Yes."

"He never finished it."

She held up the baby to him.

"May I kiss him?"

"Yes."

"He looks fine." Pepe laughed shyly. "I'm glad now. He looks wonderful."

"Take him."

"No, I'm too clumsy. You hold him."

She held the baby to her naked breast. He found the nipple and began to suck greedily. "He has a good appetite," she said.

"When do they start to talk?"

"Not for a long time."

"I want to talk to him. He is my son. I will teach him how to play on a harmonica."

She laughed.

Pepe sat down on the bed. "María, I'm all right. Everything is going to be all right. I'll get another job. Don't worry."

"I'm not worried."

AFTERWARDS

CHAIM ASKED Marcel for another cognac.

The sky was bulging with clouds. The first rains of autumn were threatening. Chaim was pleased. He enjoyed Paris in the rain. It did something for the streets.

It was almost eight, time for *apéritifs*. The terrace of the Café de Flore was crowded. The unknowing young, also their defeated elders, chattered at their tables, all looking smartly anonymous. Not yet honestly disillusioned but pretending, they idled with such intensity so as to defeat idleness itself. Along the pavement, in front of the terrace, the homosexuals passed. Always their eyes stricken, their lips waiting, as if there must be a friend or at least an enemy on the terrace, not just the others, also waiting, also pretending to be late for an appointment, not only more neurotic laughter, more sobbing in dim corners, more pink gins.

"Hey, Chaim! How about buying me another cognac?"

"Okay, Sam. But don't say I didn't warn you. You're going to die of *mal au foie*. Everybody in France does."

Sam looked brown and healthy. He had just returned from the *Côte d'Azur*, where he had spent a happy summer loafing in the sun. Not always loafing, for Sam had found time to finish his thesis. He was a young, surprisingly energetic man, and Chaim imagined he wrote well. He was big and athletic,

usually smiling or laughing, always as if he thought everything was part of a tremendous joke.

"Let's go to the races tomorrow, Chaim. David will drive
us out."

"Okay. That sounds like fun."

There were many posters on the walls. Most of them adver-
tised exhibitions, but one was a travel poster. It read: VISIT
ROME – *The scene of MGM's Quo Vadis!*

"Toni should be here soon," Sam said.

"Where are they?"

"She took the kid to the *jardins*." He looked at his watch.
"They should be home by now. She won't be long. Does she
know yet?"

"No."

"Are you going to tell her now?"

"Why not?"

"If you like I'll go. I mean if you want to be alone with her."

"No. Don't be silly."

"What are you going to do in Italy?"

"I don't know. I've got many friends there. Maybe I'll open
up a bar again? I'm tired of translating dirty novels by kids
who took a course on it in college. A bar would be fun."

"Open up a bar in Venice, Chaim. We'll all come out and
live with you."

"Soak Paris in a tub of stagnant water for maybe a thousand years and you've got Venice. I don't like it. It's too much
like a collapsed lung. I think I'll go to Florence."

"Stop off on the Côte, Chaim. You drink pink wines all
morning and sleep all afternoon. Cagnes is short on heteros,
the last one they had committed suicide in July. There's an
opening you could walk right into!"

"What are you being so goddam happy about?"

Sam took a tremendous puff of his cigar. Frowning, he
appeared almost silly. He was a naturally happy person. "I
want to marry Toni," he said. "Is that okay?"

"Why shouldn't it be okay?"

But Chaim had learnt only recently of Sam's attachment to Toni. He had had an inkling of what was coming when Sam had become a regular client of the Bar Andalucia, where Toni danced and sang *flamencos*. Sam was all right. He was a hopeful man, optimistic, and with the finest of the American qualities. Chaim had approved, but Toni still lapsed into despondency on slight provocation and Chaim had wanted to be more certain still before he committed himself. He felt that he should be cautious. What if Sam was only interested in having an affair? Yes, that's Sam's business, Chaim thought. But Toni might not be able to take it.

"What about the other guy? I know he's dead, but . . . Look, Chaim, did he commit suicide or was he murdered?"

"What does she say?"

"She's damned evasive."

"He, well, he was murdered. But he committed suicide too."

"What happened to the guy who did it?"

"He's in Western Germany now. He's very important these days. He's in on this European Army business."

"Oh!"

"Are you disappointed in me? Do you think I should have fixed him?"

"That's your business."

André was a casualty. Kraus killed him, but not for himself, he was the instrument of us all. Killing Kraus would prove nothing. In fact, you might as well get this through your head now. *Nothing is ever resolved, but it's always worth it.* If André had been a little smarter and a bit less emotional he might still be around. He's dead, and that's too bad. He might have been a great painter, he might have been a lot of things. Unfortunately he died before he reached maturity.

"He was a pretty fine person, eh, Chaim?"

"You saw the pictures that were saved."

"Do you resent me? I mean Toni . . ."

"All I ask is that you be good to her. I'll send you my address. If you need anything, write immediately. Also you must always be good to the child. That's extremely important."

"She didn't want to have it."

"She wanted it to be born dead. Thank God she's over that now. But you must be careful."

"Who's child is it? It's not his."

"If you marry her it's yours. If not, don't marry her."

"Okay. Just as you say."

"Here she is."

Toni kissed Chaim cheerfully and sat down. But he could see that something was wrong. Her eyes were red.

"I'll go and get the waiter," Sam said. "I'll be right back."

She handed Chaim a clipping. There was an old photo of Guillermo, and a story in underneath. He, and several others, were going on trial shortly. The prosecution was demanding the death penalty.

"I know," Chaim said. "I saw it yesterday."

"What will we do?"

"Things are already being done. There will be foreign observers at the trial. It doesn't mean much but at least he won't be hanged. I got him word. I offered to get him out of the country as soon as he was released. He doesn't want to come."

"Are you sure he won't be shot?"

"Yes. How's André?"

"All right, he's sleeping."

"Good."

"Chaim, let me change his name. He's beginning to look more and more like Kraus."

"Toni, stop it."

"I can't help it. When things like this happen it starts all over again."

"You're getting married, child. You'll be happy."

"Do you like him?"

She knew that Sam was after Chaim's approval and she was immensely pleased about it. Pleased, and somewhat concerned. It would be difficult (André would have said "ugly," she thought pleasurably) if Chaim didn't consent.

"Very much."

"I don't like the people who come to this café," she said suddenly.

"Toni, I'm going away. I'm going to Italy."

"Is it your passport again?"

"Yes."

"Oh, Chaim."

"You write me every week. Next summer you can both come out. I'll have a house for you. But only for the summer. You are going to be a married woman and you have your own life to lead."

"Chaim! Where will you go from Italy? How many more countries?"

"If I didn't like it I wouldn't do it. You decide to live in a certain way and you know what it's going to cost you. It's worth it. I like it."

"Chaim, is there any hope?"

"Yes, child. Of course there is."

"Is there?"

"There is always hope. Always. There has to be."

Afterword

BY TED KOTCHEFF

I have a great deal of affection for *The Acrobats*, for it was responsible for two of the closest friendships of my life.

In 1955, I was directing live television drama for the Canadian Broadcasting Corporation. Nathan Cohen was a story editor in the drama department. He is now almost forgotten, certainly under-appreciated, as I think that he was one of the few critics that attempted, through the feuilleton he published, *The Broadsheet*, to raise the level of cultural activity in Canada and judge it by the highest standards. One day, Nathan came into my office carrying a slim volume, *The Acrobats*, by a new young Canadian writer, Mordecai Richler, and urged me to read it. He said it was quite a precocious performance, and was now corresponding with the author to obtain the television rights. Further, he thought that when I went to Europe I should look him up. He thought that Mordecai and I had similar sensibilities, and was certain that he and I would become good friends. I do not know what he based this prophecy on but, of course, his intuition turned out to be completely accurate.

I read the book and was deeply impressed by its sophistication and great seriousness. That it was written by a nineteen-year-old was hard to believe. It was so assured; this was no tentative voice. He knew exactly what he was doing. It was brash and unashamed. "I may not know where I am going," he was saying, "but I am a novelist." It was certainly a young man's book, full of passion and romanticism. Youthful romanticism is commonplace. What was not commonplace was Mordecai's attempt to deal with profound issues both moral and political. Mordecai and I were almost exact contemporaries, and he was dealing with concerns that were exercising me at that time.

Mordecai did the adaptation of *The Acrobats* himself, condensing it into an hour-long television play, which was produced live by the CBC on January 13, 1957. Until recently, television had little sense of its historical value: important materials were dumped, priceless tapes were wiped to be used again. So it was with little hope that I had my brother Tim make inquiries to see if the CBC had any record of this production. Thrillingly, there was in existence an old kinescope of the show, the first production of one of Mordecai's works. The CBC generously gave me a video copy of this buried treasure. Aside from one or two interesting performances, the show is not successful. But then imagine trying to recreate Valencia in Studio "A" on Jarvis Street in Toronto. What stands out is Mordecai's adaptation. Most writers have problems adapting their own work, never being able to achieve the necessary objectivity. But one sees in this first foray into writing for television that Mordecai was a natural. Later he would blossom into a first-rate screenwriter.

The following summer, I went to the south of France. Mordecai was living in a village, Tourettes-sur-Loup, nestled in the Alpes-Maritimes. We drank in the town's only bar, a café with tables set up in the town's small square. Mordecai was taciturn, watchful, rabbinical. I did most of the talking. There was not much indication of the wit that he possessed, though at one point he asked me who my favourite novelist was. I answered, somewhat pretentiously, "Henry James."

"Then you'll be right at home with my novels, won't you." We chuckled and kept drinking.

I spent a week in Tourettes. Mordecai and I drank together when we could. We would gaze at each other in quiet assessment. As Mordecai wrote to me later, we discovered that we were "horses of the same colour." We had similar slummy backgrounds, the identical coarse adolescence. Our fathers were the same, foolish but endearing losers – his, a failed scrap dealer, mine, a milkman and failed hash slinger. How in the world did we have the ambition to become a novelist and a film director?

At the age of nineteen, a cocksure Mordecai dropped out of Sir George Williams College, cashed in a small insurance policy, and, with his Royal Portable tucked under his arm, left Canada and set out for Europe, determined to become a novelist. Ours was probably the last generation to be in the grip of that Hemingway-Fitzgerald romanticism, the fantasy that, in order to become good at any artistic activity, one had to go to Europe. Certainly, as Robert Fulford put it, we felt we had "to graduate from Canada." In 1950, the literary landscape in Canada was barren. I took a course in Canadian and American literature at the University of Toronto in 1948: one hour on a Morley Callaghan novel, one hour on a Hugh MacLennan novel, two or three hours on a few decent weekend poets, and that was it. Certainly, there was little in Canada for a budding writer to build on.

That Canadian self-deprecation we all know so well was functioning at all levels. While I was directing for the CBC, a vice-president of the Corporation said to me at a party, "Ted, you're a very talented director. If you want to develop, get out of this provincial backwater as fast as you can." And we wanted to test our talents against the best. Mordecai did not want to be known as a Canadian writer or a Jewish writer, but as *a writer*, to be measured against all other writers.

I remember that when Mordecai and I left Canada. we had a misguided contempt for those who stayed at home, and they returned the compliment by regarding us with resentment. After the years abroad, I came back to Canada to direct the film of *The Apprenticeship of Duddy Kravitz*. In the newspapers for many years afterwards, I was always referred to with the same epithet, "*émigré* Canadian director, Ted Kotcheff."

Maybe the rest of Canada had an inferiority complex, but not Mordecai or me. We went to Europe brimming with a self-confidence bordering on arrogance. I'll show those Limeys what directing's about.

London and Paris were full of Canadian and American artists. Mavis Gallant, Ted Allan, Richard Outram, one of Canada's finest living poets, and many, many others. In Paris, Mordecai hung out with a lively bunch of painters and writers. The idea was to live as cheaply as one could while writing that novel or painting that painting. Information was continually exchanged as to the most inexpensive places to live and eat, to the best black-market money-changer providing the most francs for one's bucks. On July 1, Mordecai took his chum Terry Southern to the Canadian embassy reception, where they stuffed themselves with food and drink and then stuffed their pockets with the same. On July 4, Terry took Mordecai to the American embassy for the same purpose. They all borrowed from one another. When a rich automobile heir, a Dodge or a Chrysler, came to Paris every summer to buy paintings, there was universal rejoicing. The painters would generously share in the booty with their writer friends. When Mordecai was desperate, he made demands on his father, who would come through with a few bucks – not a gift, his father insisted, but a loan, which he kept track of in a little black book.

In Paris, Mordecai devoured Malraux, Hemingway, Céline, Sartre, Camus, all of whom make guest appearances stylistically in *The Acrobats*. Many critics, including Mordecai himself, dismissed the book as being hopelessly derivative. But it seems to me entirely natural that a tyro writer should write in the style of those writers he likes to read. Besides, I enjoy pastiche. Consider the final sentences of the novel.

"Chaim, is there any hope?"
"Yes, child. Of course there is."
"Is there?"
"There is always hope. Always. There has to be."

Hemingway with a soupçon of Camus – not at all bad!

Finally, Mordecai ended up in Ibiza, Spain, where for thirty dollars a month, he rented a beautiful three-bedroom villa on the ocean, including a maid. He got down to serious work on *The Acrobats*, whose original title was *The Jew of Valencia*. And to gather authentic detail, he travelled to Valencia during its fiesta.

Mordecai went to Spain not only because it was cheap, but because it held an important place in his mythology and mine. In *Joshua Then and Now*, Part III begins:

For many members of Joshua's generation, Spain was above all a territory of the heart. A country of the imagination. Too young to have fought there, but necessarily convinced that they would have gone, proving to themselves and the essential Mr. Hemingway that they did not lack for *cojones*, it was the first political kiss. Not so much a received political idea as a moral inheritance.

When John Osborne's Jimmy Porter, in *Look Back in Anger*, mourned that there were no more good, clean causes left, Joshua glowed in his Royal Court seat, nodding yes, yes, but once there was Spain.

So Mordecai going to Spain was in no way accidental. When he arrived, the Civil War had been over only a very short time, and through what he found there he was able to dramatize his political feelings, and by writing his novel – like André with his art – come to some kind of understanding.

In Ibiza, Mordecai hung out with a raffish bunch of Spaniards, including the madame of the local brothel, Rosita, who makes an appearance in the novel, name unchanged (and in *Joshua Then and Now*). Mordecai would have wild drinking parties at his house that lasted the whole night through. The Spanish secret police became suspicious of him. Why was he not behaving like a tourist? Why was he doing all these non-tourist things like partying with priapic gypsy dancers, whores, madames, fishermen, riff-raff? The secret police were paranoid about all foreigners then, and they may have thought Mordecai was consorting with Republicans. Was he a communist, an anarchist? Also, there was a German living in Ibiza, an ex-member of the Wehrmacht, whom Mordecai kept making inquiries about, asking questions at the local *quitapena*, gathering possible source material. The secret police started to hassle him, making it difficult to work, and so he left and returned to Paris, where he finished the novel. Mordecai deals with his Ibiza experience at some length in *Joshua Then and Now*, and it's worth reading it in relation to *The Acrobats*.

I lived in Spain in the mid-fifties, near Malaga, trying to be a poet. I can attest to the marvellous way Mordecai has captured in the novel the Spain of that time: what it looked like, what it felt like, its sounds, and its smells, the cripples, the begging children, the old men searching for butts, the blind lottery sellers, the whores, the pickpockets, the unemployed, the gypsies, the police spies, the Guardia Civil with their comic-opera patent-leather hats, the flotsam and jetsam of two wars, the foreigners, the sour cream of Europe, or, as Ken Tynan, who was also there at the time, described them, "The Nescafé Society." There was a pervasive atmosphere of intense sensuality and sexual abandon that Mordecai delineates with great accuracy. One of the central themes of the novel is the destructive power of Eros. All the characters are in its grip and their lives are irrevocably altered or destroyed by it.

There are some extraordinary set pieces in *The Acrobats* executed with great descriptive power: the brothel sequence, a bar at closing time, the ruined port by moonlight, the Valencia slums, and, best of all, the mad, frenzied, Dionysian dance in the streets of the poor, the unemployed, the whores. Shaking, stomping, clapping, trying to drink and dance their "spiritpain" away. The dance is intercut with a group of the rich and powerful, a smug upper-class visiting American lady, the fatuous American ambassador, a corrupt archbishop, and a reactionary general who look down, with total purblindness, on the people in the street. The satirical contrapuntal intercutting between the two opposite worlds in a John Dos Passos cinematic collage is one of the triumphs of the book and demonstrates Mordecai's understanding and deep feeling for the deprived and downtrodden.

At that time Mordecai was a struggling young political ideologue and, like André, in a state of intellectual turmoil and uncertainty. It is in this regard that André is the most transparent projection of Mordecai. André is part of the postwar generation caught between the proponents of a faltering revolution and the remnants of a dying culture. He feels abandoned by his ideological mentors who cheered the revolution in the thirties and now have gone over to the enemy, democratic capitalism, thus declaring themselves morally and intellectually bankrupt. André strongly feels the necessity to believe in something and act on it, for not to act is to be as good as dead. Guillermo accuses him of "being without hope or reason or direction." But the communism Guillermo urges on André has two faces: on the one hand its idealism represented by Guillermo, and on the other its cynical, ruthless Stalinism represented by Manuelo. It's the Manuelos who make it impossible for humanists like André and Mordecai to join the party, no matter how much they sympathize with its goal to end poverty and injustice. André knows what he's against but not what he's for. In this state of social and political paralysis, and in a deep depression about the future, he is drinking himself to death. No answers are provided; only at the end of the book is a fragile expression of unsubstantiated hope offered up.

Toni's cure for André's predicament is for him to leave the "sadness of Europe" and return to Canada: "We will have a fine home in the mountains. He shall have a room full of books and I shall sew for our children in the parlour." Interestingly, this is exactly what Mordecai did when he returned to Canada from England in 1972 with his wife, Florence, and their children, and went to live on Lake Magog in Quebec's Eastern Townships. Toni's fantasy, however, was not Florence's. Mordecai had to drag her away from London's sophistications to that Canadian bucolic retreat.

A concomitant theme to the politics in the book is an examination of the relationship between art and society. Whom will André paint for? Guillermo attempts to recruit André to paint for the proletariat and "reach an audience so far untouched. You wouldn't have to paint for the fatuous corrupt bourgeois." André has a contract to sell his paintings in New York. But is this what he wants, pleasing alien tastes? André never resolves his dilemma and declares rather disingenuously. "I paint for the understanding," hoping that "painting will explain to me what I am looking for." Mordecai always hated the dehumanizing compartmentalization of people into classes. In the sixties I was involved with a group of left-wing playwrights and directors called Centre 42, and we took art and theatre to the working classes in cities all over England. Mordecai was scathing in his disapproval of what I was doing. So the issue obviously resonated long and loud in his politics.

Ignoring the old chestnut of only writing about what you know, Mordecai deals with several Spanish characters, and I find his depiction of them vivid and convincing, no small feat for a neophyte writer. Mordecai has a great ability to empathize with all his characters, even the repellent Krauses. Barney is ridiculed for his crassness and simple-minded political attitudes. Yet, as he did later with Duddy Kravitz (and Barney in some ways is an early sketch of Duddy), Mordecai gets under Barney's skin and manages to enlist one's sympathies for him. As André says, one should aspire "to be capable of empathy, to understand the failings of a man – even as you condemn him." This is a clear statement of Mordecai's life-long artistic credo.

What strikes me most forcibly in rereading the novel now is that there is not a scintilla of humour in it. Nowhere do we see that Rabelaisian ribaldry that was to characterize Mordecai's later work and make him one of the funniest writers of the twentieth century. Coming from a non-literary background, the young Mordecai probably felt that humour was inappropriate; one must be "literary" and write a book like a book ought to be. He saw himself as a serious writer and interpreter of life. Further, there was a refusal to believe that his background was worth writing about or could be of any literary interest whatsoever. It was not until *The Apprenticeship of Duddy Kravitz* that Mordecai hit his stride and realized that St. Urbain Street was what Yoknapatawpha County was to William Faulkner, his authorial turf that he was destined to write about. Now and then, though, Mordecai the future satirist shows his mordant teeth with a swipe at Canadian Kultchir (sic), "mediocrity draped in the maple leaf," and in the aforementioned John Dos Passos sequence.

The other characteristic of *The Acrobats* that surprises me is its unique poetic style, its pyrotechnical display of verbal virtuosity, its feverish onomatopoeia effects, its overwrought similes: "Lamp posts like the luminous yellow spittle of gnarled immobile cripples," or "Buildings, like bloated lungs gasping." In the middle of the street-dance sequence, there is a sudden burst of poetic prose:

> I shall walk up to heaven and turn off the stars one by one. I shall rub out the Milky Way with my heel and paint the moon in black. I shall kick the sun sizzling into the sea and I shall spit comets on all of Spain. If God is in I shall tell him why.

Throughout, there is a youthful explosion of words, and one senses Mordecai's delight in flexing his verbal muscles. Of course, in his subsequent work, perhaps under the influence of one of our culture heroes, Isaac Babel, who urged writers to strip away adjectives and adverbs, Mordecai's style was entirely different: his prose was lean, edgy, unadorned, controlled. His wilder flights of fancy went into his comedic inventions. So this book represents, stylistically, the road not taken, a rejected novelistic persona.

In the ensuing years, Mordecai affected embarrassment about this novel, laughed about it, and congratulated himself on keeping it out of print. But whatever the novel's callow defects and gaucheries, I think it is important that it be reconsidered. Florence still disagrees with her husband and has approved its reprinting, feeling it would be a grievous mistake to deprive the serious reader of this early book. If one wants to follow his artistic trajectory, reading *The Acrobats* is obligatory. This is the first moment when he takes off on his journey as a writer. And there is a connection between this novel and the high seriousness of *Solomon Gursky Was Here*, which, in my opinion, is Mordecai's masterpiece. But one ought not to read *The Acrobats* for merely literary and historical reasons but for the many novelistic pleasures it provides.

And the young Mordecai reveals a lot about himself in *The Acrobats*, much more than in any of his other books, where he masks himself behind novelistic objectivity. André possesses Mordecai's inner intense emotionality, but I see more of Mordecai in the wandering Jewish philosopher Chaim. He shares with Chaim a melancholy sense of life's impossibility, its ineradicable injustices, and this understanding leads to a deep wellspring of compassion for the victims of the human condition. Perhaps Mordecai was embarrassed about this book because he appears too nakedly in it.

When Mordecai finished the book in Paris, he was almost twenty-one. Now the search for a publisher began. With the assistance of a friend, Michael Sayers, he came to be represented by a British agent, a delightfully eccentric woman, Joyce Weiner. She loved Mordecai like a son and she dedicated herself to getting *The Acrobats* published. There were a number of rejections by various publishers, however, and it was with some sense of failure that he quit Europe and returned to Montreal. But suddenly, the British publisher André Deutsch, under the auspices of the perspicacious Diane Athill, agreed to publish the book and, subsequently, it was taken by Putnam for the United States. Mordecai received, respectively, 100 pounds and 750 dollars. The book was not published in Canada, though Collins distributed the British version. Mordecai left for London once more.

The Acrobats received many respectable reviews in Great Britain and Canada, and several critics recognized its promise and the makings of an important and original writer. But in spite of these reviews, the book had no commercial success. It was translated into several European languages: Danish, German, Norwegian, and Swedish. Ironically, considering the depiction of the two German characters in it, Mordecai had his greatest success with this novel in Germany, where, a year later, he was lionized and had his first taste of literary fame.

I asked Mordecai about the source of the title, and he told me it came from Rilke – or was it Lorca? In any case, the metaphor, as it applies to the book's precariously balanced characters, is perfect.

Although *The Acrobats* was Mordecai's first published novel, it was not his first novel – something I discovered in the early sixties. Mordecai and I shared a flat in Swiss Cottage, London, in the late fifties, when he was writing *The Apprenticeship of Duddy Kravitz*. Sitting in the living room was a half-size metal steamer trunk perpetually covered with magazines and boxes. It belonged to Mordecai, and so I never inquired about its contents. Mordecai moved out to live with Florence, and then I left for a more commodious flat for myself and Sylvia Kay, who was soon to become my wife. Shortly afterwards, the house was demolished to make way for a swimming bath.

Some years later, Mordecai came to me and asked where that steamer trunk was. The University of Calgary was buying all his papers and correspondence and the trunk had his first novel in it and some early short stories. "It would be worth a tidy sum – you know, juvenilia." I said, "I thought you took it." He said, "I thought you kept it." We searched our premises and our memories, but what happened to it was a total mystery – a mystery that was never solved. After reproaching him for never telling me what was in it, I asked him what the novel was about, but he said it was not worth talking about, dismissing it as a poor adolescent effort. The only inkling I got was once, when we came out of seeing Fellini's *I Vitelloni*, we were discussing its merits and Mordecai said that the film was like the obligatory first novel that every writer feels compelled to do – "how I suffered in the oppressive, stultifying atmosphere of a provincial city and finally discovered the courage to leave for the big city." In the way that he said it, I suddenly had a flash that he was referring to that lost novel, but I have no real evidence, only that unsubstantiated intuition. Mordecai never mentioned it again.

I began this piece asserting that *The Acrobats* was responsible for *two* close friendships of mine. The second one was Florence. At the time *The Acrobats* was published, she was married to the writer Stanley Mann; they were part of the Canadian contingent in London. At the nuptial party thrown by Ted and Kate Allan for Mordecai the day before his marriage to Cathy Boudreau, Mordecai could not keep his eyes off Florence. He was mesmerized by her beauty, her intelligence, her dignity. Florence took great exception to his brazen manner, and when he came over to her and inquired whether she had read *The Acrobats* and her reaction to it, Florence, in a very haughty and frosty manner, replied, "Yes. I've read it. I liked it, but not enough to want to meet its author." Of course, far from deterring Mordecai, this only inflamed him.

Somewhat later, he and I left another social occasion where Florence was present, and Mordecai said, "She's mine. I want her." "Mordecai, she's married, you're married. Are you crazy?" "I don't care. I want her and I'm going to take her." When both their marriages ruptured, Florence let him do so, and she came into my life as well – the best friend one could ask for.

BY MORDECAI RICHLER

ESSAYS

Hunting Tigers Under Glass: Essays and Reports (1968)
Shovelling Trouble (1972)
Notes on an Endangered Species and Others (1974)
The Great Comic Book Heroes and Other Essays (1978)
Home Sweet Home: My Canadian Album (1984)
Broadsides: Reviews and Opinions (1990)
Belling the Cat: Essays, Reports, and Opinions (1998)

FICTION

The Acrobats (1954)
Son of a Smaller Hero (1955)
A Choice of Enemies (1957)
The Apprenticeship of Duddy Kravitz (1959)
The Incomparable Atuk (1963)
Cocksure (1968)
The Street (1969)
St. Urbain's Horseman (1971)
Joshua Then and Now (1980)
Solomon Gursky Was Here (1989)
Barney's Version (1997)

FICTION FOR YOUNG ADULTS
Jacob Two-Two Meets the Hooded Fang (1975)
Jacob Two-Two and the Dinosaur (1987)
Jacob Two-Two's First Spy Case (1995)

HISTORY
Oh Canada! Oh Quebec!:
Requiem for a Divided Country (1992)
This Year in Jerusalem (1994)

SPORTS
On Snooker (2001)
Dispatches from the Sporting Life (2002)

TRAVEL
Images of Spain (1977)